Food Rules!

THE STUFF YOU MUNCH, ITS CRUNCH, ITS PUNCH, AND WHY YOU SOMETIMES LOSE YOUR LUNCH

by BILL HADUCH

illustrated by RICK STROMOSKI

DUTTON CHILDREN'S BOOKS · NEW YORK

Special thanks to:

Bernadette Garchinsky Janas, Ph.D., R.D.
Director, Dietetics Program, Rutgers University

Acknowledgments

Jess Brallier; Lee Gutkind; Meredith Mundy Wasinger and her mystery friend;
Marcia Wernick; Laurin Lucaire; Karen Lotz; Amy Wick; Cindy Kearney;
Sarah Longstreet; Rosetta Merritt; Lew Migal; Tom Stevens; Diane Kress, R.D.;
Karl Skutski; Antonio Carlos Jobim; John, Paul, George, and Ringo

Library of Congress Cataloging-in-Publication Data
Haduch, Bill.
Food Rules: the stuff you munch, its crunch, its punch,
and why you sometimes lose your lunch/by Bill Haduch;
illustrated by Rick Stromoski.—1st ed. p. cm
Includes bibliographical references and index.
ISBN 0-525-46419-0
1. Food—Composition—Juvenile literature.
[1. Food. 2. Nutrition.] I. Stromoski, Rick, ill. II. Title
TX551.H23 2001 613.2—dc21 00-042698

Published in the United States by Dutton Children's Books,
a division of Penguin Putnam Books for Young Readers
345 Hudson Street, New York, New York 10014
www.penguinputnam.com
Designed by Ellen M. Lucaire
Printed in Hong Kong • First Edition
3 5 7 9 10 8 6 4

For Nita, Will, and Casey,
Adventurous Eaters all
—B.H.

For Molly and Danna
—R.S.

Contents

"FIRST WE EAT, THEN WE DO EVERYTHING ELSE."

—M.F.K. Fisher, food-loving author who wrote *How to Cook a Wolf*

Doesn't it seem like *everything* is about food? Summer picnics. Afterschool snacks. Shopping carts. Hot-dog carts. Cafeteria lines. The ice-cream man. A frying pan. A birthday cake. Macaroni and cheese. Burgers. Fries. The butcher. The baker. The candlestick-maker. Oops . . .

Okay. *Almost* everything is about food.

We tell time with food:

> *When? After lunch!*

We fight about food:

> *I do not want green eggs and ham!*

We fight *with* food:

> *Never, ever trust a clown with a pie...*

We make noise with food:

> *Braaaaap, toot!*

We tease our friends with food:

> *You are such a hot dog!*

Favorite International Pizza Toppings
Poland: Cabbage

And yet, how much do you really know about food? Did you know that the energy in a candy bar actually comes from outer space? Did you know that most people in the world love to eat bugs? Do you know what to eat when nobody's home? Or do you just stuff your face with Krusty Kadoodle Flappers "as seen on TV!"?

Well, pull up a chair. Sit down. Grab a napkin. We're about to dig into some of the most mouthwatering stories, jokes, rumors, and facts you never knew about food. And yes, it's okay to eat while you read.

* If you lump it all together, you spend more than fifteen full days a year doing nothing but eating.
* If you *dump* it all together, you spend almost four full days a year doing nothing but going to the bathroom.
* The world's favorite flavor is chocolate.
* A scientist who tried to taste as many different animals as possible said the worst is *mole meat.*
* A single chocolate chip gives you enough energy to walk about 150 feet.
* There are about 800 kernels on an ear of corn.
* Every year, you eat about 170 grocery bags of food. (How many do you help carry? Hmmmm?)
* Food, as you know it, never actually enters your body—only the food's molecules do.
* Fewer than half the world's people use a fork, knife, and spoon to eat. The rest use chopsticks, just a knife, or just their hands.
* The world's favorite snack food is popcorn.

Humans are the only earthly beings that cook their food. Every other species eats food raw. Reasons for cooking include killing bacteria and parasites, making food more digestible, and helping food taste better. Oh, and because we have stoves.

Not Hungry? Don't Worry...

ou will be. Just a little while from now, you'll begin to feel something just under your rib cage. It may seem like a little pressure or warmth. Some people think it feels like hollowness. Others describe it as something moving around or shrinking in there. Some people even think they hear hunger's rumbling, grumbling sound effects.

You've been getting hungry every few hours since the day you were born. Isn't it about time to understand what's going on?

Don't blame an empty stomach. Early in the twentieth century, doctors noticed something interesting about patients who had their stomachs surgically removed. The patients still felt hunger the same old way. So doctors and scientists decided the feeling of hunger must come from somewhere else.

Why couldn't the teddy bear eat?
Because he was stuffed!

It turned out to be a tiny area, about the size of a garbanzo bean, in the middle of your brain. It's called the hypothalamus (hi-po-THAL-a-mus). It constantly monitors what's going on in your bloodstream and sends reports to different parts of your brain.

Blood's too warm? Make 'em sweat. Blood's too cool? Make 'em shiver. Not enough fuel in the blood? Make 'em eat. How? By making 'em hungry. It's your brain creating that unmistakable feeling called hunger.

Hunger is powerful, and it's meant to be unpleasant. Once it starts, there's really nothing you can do to relieve it except eat. And so you eat—usually until a second part of your hypothalamus tells your brain that the amount of fuel in your blood is just about right.

Hunger is not really related to the amount of food in your stomach. And the funny growling is just air getting squeezed around. You can have an empty, howling stomach and feel completely fine, as long as your hypothalamus is satisfied. Ahhhh! There is nothing, nothing like a happy hypothalamus.

Babies—they're different

From day one, babies know how to satisfy an unhappy hypothalamus. They simply cry. Almost immediately, nice people stuff something in their mouths—like a sippy cup, a spoonful of applesauce, a cracker. It's a great system and very efficient. Now that you're older, here's a little experiment. The next time you're hungry, just cry. Cry louder and louder. Really wail. Measure how long it takes before someone tries to stuff something in your mouth. Like a sock.

Sliced bread was first sold in 1928, so saying "It's the greatest thing since sliced bread" is like saying "It's the greatest thing since 1928!"

Thirst Aid

Parched? That's all in your head, too. Well, in your hypothalamus. This busy little bean, more powerful than any computer chip (so far), also checks your blood for the right balance of water. If there's not enough or if it's the wrong mixture, your brain hears all about it. Then your brain creates that dry feeling in your throat and in the back of your mouth. Soon you're clenching your throat and crawling around on your hands and knees murmuring "water, water" and seeing mirages of cool mountain streams at the front of your classroom. There's more on the joys of water in chapter 4.

What's More Impressive?

THE GARBANZO BEAN
(Actual size)

Also called the chickpea. Delightful when mashed with olive oil and lemon juice to make the Middle Eastern dish called hummus. Great for dips. (Nerds, geeks, and regular people like it, too.)

THE HYPOTHALAMUS
(Actual size)

Found deep inside your brain. Automatically monitors your blood for most of your body's survival factors—heat, cold, fuel materials, etc. Works 24 hours a day, 365 days a year, all your life. When it finds something out of balance, it works with the brain to make adjustments. (To make you hungry for hummus, for example.)

You Will Not Believe What Your Brain Wants You to Eat

ow you know *why* you're hungry. So what are you hungry *for*?
A Goofyburger? A bowl of mac and cheese? A kumquat?

Whatever you *think* you want, your brain is really screaming out for PEA SOUP. Well, not exactly, but the stuff *looks* like pea soup. It's called chyme (KIME, rhymes with *slime*), and it's a watery, greenish, brownish blend of everything you eat. Whether it's eggs or garbanzo beans or grasshoppers, everything you eat gets ground up and dissolved into this chyme, and it looks nothing like the food you just ate. (Unless you just ate pea soup!)

You can dine splendidly at the snootiest restaurant in Paris or you can sit on a curb by the post office and eat out of a paper bag. It doesn't matter. Anything you eat gets turned into green, slimy chyme, your body's favorite meal.

Did you hear about that new restaurant on the moon? The food is great, but the place has no atmosphere.

Making Chyme

The first step in making chyme is mashing whatever food you put in your mouth into tiny pieces. Chewing, that is. Your teeth and tongue grind and move the food all over your mouth, and six glands pump saliva into the mixture. The saliva wets the concoction and helps it slide down your throat when you swallow.

About ten seconds after you swallow, the mass of spitty, chewed-up food, now called the bolus (Greek for *lump*), enters your stomach. Here, powerful stomach acids attack the poor bolus, kill bacteria, and try to dissolve food chunks into the tiniest possible pieces. At the same time, your merciless stomach muscles squeeze the helpless bolus until most of it is *liquefied*. Yep, your stomach acid and stomach muscles can turn the proudest, toughest hunk of horse meat into liquid in just a few minutes. About twenty to thirty minutes after you eat, your body really begins to get fed. It's *chyme time*!

Using Chyme

A little at a time, the liquid chyme squirts out of your stomach and into your small intestine. If you've ever seen a car-wash tunnel, you have some idea what goes on in here. It's a hose-fest. Bile, a bitter liquid made by your liver and stored in your gallbladder, pours in to break down blobs of fats into smaller blobs. Juice containing sodium bicarbonate (yep, baking soda) flows in from your pancreas (PANK-kree-us) to make the stomach acid harmless. Your pancreas also dumps in a stew of enzymes that break down and rearrange the liquid chyme even further—into molecules.

Molecules are the only things that your body can really use. That's what digestion is all about—making a slush of molecules that your body can use for energy and for growth and repair.

Now, here's the real action part. These molecules, now called nutrients, are so tiny that they can pass through the walls of your small intestine and into your blood vessels. Here they go for the ride of their lives, shooting through the thousands of miles of blood vessels that twist and turn through your body. (An adult's body has about 60,000 miles of blood vessels in it.)

The nutrients whiz to your muscles to be used as fuel. They whiz to that scrape on your knee to build new skin. They whiz to your scalp to make hair. They whiz to your bone and muscle tissue to help you grow. All the while, your hypothalamus is up there in your brain, watching what's whizzing by. And if it's not happy, you get hungry.

Adults don't really have 60,000 miles of blood vessels. Do they?
Yes, they do.

But . . . but. That would stretch more than two times around the world! How can that be?
It's easy. Arteries, veins, and capillaries—some thinner than a hair—twist and turn to bring nutrients to every cell of your body. You're growing some right now. Think a few good molecules might help?

Into the Tunnel of Food

It's pretty simple, really. From your mouth through your stomach to your butt, your whole digestive system is just a thirty-foot-long food tunnel. It's wide open except for your lips and five little "gates" that open and close along the way, called sphincters (SFINK-ters). You have sphincters at your stomach's entrance and exit, one where your small intestine meets your large intestine, and two in Uranus—er, your anus. Your salivary glands, liver, gallbladder, and pancreas all squirt stuff into the tunnel to turn food into molecules that can pass through the walls of your intestines and into your bloodstream.

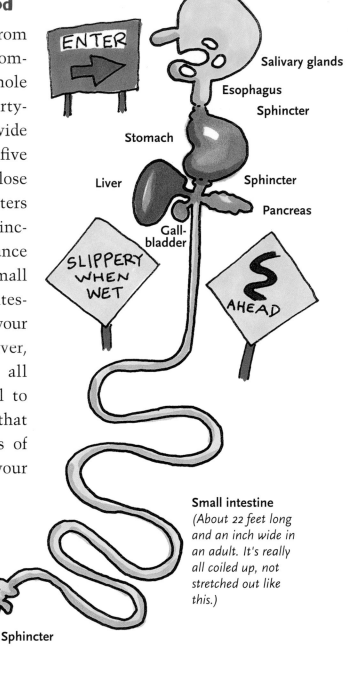

ENTER

Salivary glands

Esophagus

Sphincter

Stomach

Liver

Sphincter

Gall-
bladder

Pancreas

SLIPPERY WHEN WET

AHEAD

Small intestine
(About 22 feet long and an inch wide in an adult. It's really all coiled up, not stretched out like this.)

EXIT

Anus

Two sphincters

Sphincter

Large intestine
(About five feet long and 2 1/2 inches wide)

You Are *Not* What You Eat

What your body really uses for energy, growth, and repair are molecules—the tiniest particles of chemical substances that can still be identified as chemicals. Eat cookies and milk, and your body rearranges everything depending on what it needs. Sometimes you get a completely

new combination of molecules that weren't even in the cookies *or* the milk. People didn't always know this. Warriors going into battle would eat the meat of strong, courageous animals to try to get strength and courage. But their muscles just wanted molecules. Eating grasshoppers may have worked just as well.

Perhaps We Should All Wear "Hazardous Materials" Labels

Hydrochloric (hi-dro-KLOR-ic) acid is nasty stuff. The government has issued a five-page hazard warning all about it. It will eat through most metals and is considered one of the most difficult acids to handle because it can dissolve its container. Bricklayers use it to dissolve hardened concrete. And your stomach uses it every day to help turn your food into chyme. Fortunately, the inside of your stomach is lined with special skin and a protective layer of mucus. Otherwise, the hydrochloric acid would eat through your stomach and who knows what else? Your skin? Your clothes? The chair? The floor? Yow. Keep your acid to yourself, please.

You're So Spitty . . .

Spit. Yuck. Right? Well, no, not exactly. You need saliva to wet the food you eat. It comes out of glands in your mouth, and it's mostly water with a little mucus and minerals. Every day you produce enough to fill almost three soda cans. Making saliva really starts in your brain. Think about food, and the spit starts to flow. There's an old spitty experiment a lot of people still talk about. It's called Pavlov's Dogs. For a while Dr. Ivan Pavlov would ring a bell just before he fed his dogs. The dogs would drool for the food. Later, he found that whenever they heard a bell, the dogs would drool just *thinking* about the food. Then the telephone was invented, and all Pavlov's dogs went insane. Ha, ha. Just kidding. But the experiment part is true.

Recipe for Making Prime Chyme Slime Every Time!

Great! You just knocked off a big bag of Purple Puffy Puff Pods, and now you realize your body wants some *nutrition* in this green molecular chyme slime. What's supposed to go into this dreck? Luckily, <u>Food *Rules!*</u> has the recipe you need every day:

PRIME CHYME

5 parts carbohydrates
about 1 part or less fats
1 part proteins
a sprinkling of vitamins and minerals
about two quarts of water

Mix well and enjoy!

A hundred years ago, <u>Good Housekeeping</u> magazine often offered recipes for heart, tripe, sweetbreads, and kidneys.

Fats? Proteins? You mean you've never seen a bag just labeled "Carbohydrates" at your local supermarket?

That's because bodies are designed to make chyme from food. But what kind of food? And how much? If you look at your wrist, you'll probably see a watch, not a food gauge. How can you ever know whether you're putting the right amount of carbohydrates, fats, or anything else into your chyme?

Here's the secret: All we can really do is take good guesses every day at what to eat and how much of each thing. The more you know about food, the better guesses you'll make. The better guesses you make, the better your body will work. It's always good to know the inside scoop on what makes good chyme.

THE INSIDE SCOOP ON CARBOHYDRATES— AS COMPLEX AS POSSIBLE, PLEASE

Carbohydrates come from plants—vegetables; grains such as wheat, corn, oats, and barley; beans; and fruits. Your body is designed to get most of its energy from eating carbohydrates.

Right now, your brain and all your muscles, from your eyes to your heart to your toes, are being fueled by a simple carbohydrate—a type of sugar. No, it's not quite the stuff in your sugar bowl, but almost. Your body's fuel is a sugar called glucose, and if you were to taste it, it would seem about half as sweet as regular table sugar.

Now get ready for the fun part. The energy in glucose actually comes from outer space—it starts out as the sun's energy. When the sun shines on plants here on Earth, they store the energy by making glucose molecules. In a plant's structure, the glucose molecules form long, complex chains, sometimes *1,000 links long*. This is what people mean by "complex carbohydrates."

When you eat food with complex carbohydrates—say potatoes or whole grains —digestion has to break down these complex chains into single molecules of glucose that can pass through the intestine's wall and into your bloodstream. This takes time, and that's good. While the glucose links are breaking off the long chains, your blood is getting a nice, steady stream of energy. You've got one very happy hypothalamus up there.

In many foods with simple carbohydrates, the sugar company has already broken up the complex chains for you. For example, the carbohydrate chains in your sugar bowl are only *two links long*! It's sugar. It's sweet. People and many animals are very attracted to it. So what's the problem?

Well, when you eat a whole bag of Purple Puffy Puff Pods, or anything with a lot of sugar in it, your chyme gets loaded with many, many two-link carbohydrate chains. During digestion, all these short chains break very quickly into single links of glucose. And all these glucose molecules dump right into your bloodstream. It's like a flood of instant energy. For the first few minutes your hypothalamus is pleased, and you feel good. But soon the flood drives your hypothalamus *crazy*! Too much glucose in the blood, it tells your brain. Your brain commands your liver and muscles to capture the glucose molecules and store them for later use. Suddenly your blood has less glucose in it than you started with. And you have less energy than you started with. You begin to feel exhausted and hungry. Maybe even cranky.

At this point, many people simply reach for another bag of sugar-coated Purple Puffy Puff Pods, and the whole thing starts all over again.

Blame It on the Candy Bar
Microwave cooking was discovered in 1946 when a scientist turned on a magnetron tube and accidentally melted a candy bar in his pocket.

Sugar in Disguise

You'll see the following ingredients on many food packages. All are sugar—simple carbohydrates that make things sweet and turn almost instantly into energy in your body: corn syrup, high-fructose corn syrup, fructose, maltose, molasses, fruit juice concentrate, brown sugar, invert sugar, corn sweetener, lactose, raw sugar, glucose (also called dextrose), table sugar (also called sugar or sucrose), syrup, and honey.

A Taste of Energy

To get an idea of what glucose tastes like, try a teaspoon of corn syrup. It's often in food stores near the pancake syrups and flour. Glucose (or dextrose) is usually listed as the main ingredient. It's also one of the sweeteners in sports drinks like Gatorade. And next time you see hospital patients with IV needles stuck in their arms, guess what's often dripping into their bloodstreams, drop by drop, to give them a measured amount of energy? *Glucose!*

Full and Happy

Scientists at the University of Sydney in Australia studied which foods keep people and their hypothalamuses happiest the longest. Here's some of what they found out about carbohydrate foods:

* In a typical serving size, plain baked potatoes keep a person satisfied almost five times longer than doughnuts.

* Whole-grain bread is 50 percent more satisfying than white bread.

* Popcorn is twice as filling as a candy bar.

Just Passing Through

Getting glucose by digesting complex carbohydrates is really the best way to get steady energy. But complex carbohydrates are also great for something you *can't* digest. Fiber. Fiber makes up the bodies of plants. Your body can't break it down into molecules, so it never gets into your bloodstream. It just moves along in your intestines, gathering debris and helping to sweep things out. Fiber is so disgustingly cool that it gets its own chapter.

A pineapple has nothing to do with pines or apples. It gets its name from the Spanish word piña meaning "pinecone," because it sort of looks like one.

Worried if you swallow gum it'll stay in your stomach for seven years?

The truth is a piece or two of swallowed gum will pass right through your digestive system like fiber. But beware of swallowing huge wads. They can get stuck and have to be surgically removed.

THE INSIDE SCOOP ON FAT—
YOUR GREASY FRIEND

You can't live without fat. You know, the slippery, gloppy stuff you get from foods like meat, fish, milk, butter, cheese, nuts, and vegetable oils.

Fat waterproofs your body's cells. Like a battery, it stores energy—your body can convert it to glucose. It can store twice as much energy as protein can. It gives your body parts protective cushions, sometimes attractive ones. It even makes up most of your brain and helps your brain move information around. Honest. Your brain is mostly a big blob of fat and fatty acids. So let's give your brain a workout. Let's play Pick Your Favorite Fat!

* **Saturated fat.** Most of it comes from animal foods and tends to be solid at room temperature, like butter. When saturated fat comes from tropical plants like coconuts, it's more like oil. Some scientists worry that eating too much saturated fat for too long can help clog blood vessels.

* **Unsaturated fat.** These include polyunsaturated (polly-un-SATCH-er-rated) and monounsaturated (mono-un-SATCH-er-rated) fats. It's usually an oil and comes from plants like olives, corn, and soybeans, and from seafood. Some scientists believe that eating these types of fats instead of the saturated kind can help some people *avoid* clogged blood vessels.

* **Trans fats, or partially hydrogenated oils.** These are created when liquid vegetable oils are hardened to make some margarines and shortenings. Trans fats are used in all kinds of baked goods and snack foods. Scientists now believe eating too much trans fats for too long can help clog blood vessels.

Okay, time's up. If you picked unsaturated fat as your favorite fat, then you're using your fat-filled brain wisely.

Hey, What About Calories?

When people think of fat, they think of calories. They're afraid of calories. They run from calories. They don't even know what calories are. Well, here's the unscary truth: Calories are just a way to measure how much energy a food can give you after you eat it. It's like looking at some fire logs and saying, "This log will burn for four minutes, but this one will burn for nine minutes." Fat is like the nine-minute log. It has more calories than carbohydrates or protein. But it's usually not ready for immediate use. It tends to go into storage while your body uses carbohydrates (glucose) for energy first.

Speaking of Calories . . .

Because people are so afraid of fat and calories, companies try to make money by selling "fat-free" this, "no-calorie" that, and "lite" everything else. It's easy for people to get the idea that all fat and calories are bad. Rumors spread about amazing diets. "Eat nothing but grapefruit!" they say. "Eat nothing but celery!" "Eat nothing at all! Period!" Well, the truth is you need hundreds of calories a day just to keep your heart pumping and your lungs sucking air. And without any fat, your brain doesn't work. Cut way back on fat and calories without knowing what you're doing, and you could wind up sick or damaged or (insert horror-movie organ music here) *among the dearly departed*!

Cholesterol: Another Scary Monster

Boo! Cholesterol (kuh-LESS-ster-all) might scare even more people than calories do. Cholesterol is not even a fat. It's a waxy substance made by your liver. It travels through your blood and helps build, repair, and waterproof your cells. Your liver usually makes enough to keep you healthy. In food, cholesterol is often found mixed in with saturated fats. Some people worry that if they eat too much saturated fat for too many years, the extra cholesterol will help clog their blood vessels. And while trans fats don't have cholesterol, new research has shown that over time, trans fats may help cholesterol do its clogging. *Yeeesh!* Thanks a lot!

Five Favorite Nicknames for the Human Mouth:

potato slot   pie hole

bazoo

yap

trap

THE INSIDE SCOOP ON PROTEIN— FINELY CHOPPED, THEN DESTROYED

You get protein from meat, fish, eggs, poultry, dairy products, vegetables, beans, nuts, and whole grains. Everyone talks about how protein builds muscles and blood vessels and skin and hair, and helps make things happen in your body. But here's a little twist: It's not really the same protein that's in your food.

Nope. Digestion demolishes that protein beyond recognition. What's left in the chyme are those proteins' building blocks—the amino (uh-ME-no) acids. Your body then rearranges these amino acids, often swapping them with other foods in the chyme to build custom-made proteins just for you. That's one of the reasons it's so important to eat a wide variety of foods.

Only twenty kinds of amino acids combine to make all the thousands of kinds of proteins in your body. (Sort of how only twenty-six letters combine to make all the words in this book.) Amino acids are chemicals, and they have chemical names like valine and lysine. There's no difference between the valine that's in a hot dog and the valine that's in a potato.

About nine of these twenty amino acids are considered "essential"

Mom: Eat your spinach, Howie. It'll put color in your cheeks.

Howie: But Mom, who wants green cheeks?

amino acids. These are the *basic* building blocks. You need to eat all nine, or your body generally can't make its own protein. Meats, fish, dairy products, eggs—food we get from animals—include all nine essential amino acids. This means they have complete protein.

Most foods we get from plants don't have all nine. One vegetable may include six essential amino acids, and another vegetable may include five. By combining these vegetables, you can cover all nine, but it can be a bit tricky. That's why people who decide to be vegetarians need to do some research. Show your folks this book. Read other books. Ask your doctor or a nutritionist. You need to make sure your chyme has building blocks you can use. After all, hair is protein, and nobody likes a bad hair *year*.

For the Hard-Core Curious . . .

If you really, really want to know, here's a list of all twenty amino acids used to make the thousands of proteins in the human body. Those in red are often considered the nine essential amino acids: alanine, arginine, asparagine, aspartic acid, cysteine, glutamic acid, glutamine, glycine, histidine, isoleucine, leucine, lysine, methionine, phenylalanine, proline, serine, threonine, tryptophan, tyrosine, valine. Don't worry, there's no quiz. Yet.

Soy & Quinoa: Plants with Protein Power

A few plants *do* have complete protein with all nine essential amino acids. The most popular right now is soybeans. When you eat foods made from soybeans, you get many of the benefits of meat without any saturated fats or cholesterol. And though soy doesn't give you all of meat's other nutrients, it has substances that may actually help prevent diseases like cancer. There's no doubt soy products will become more and more popular in years to come. Look for soy "milk" and tofu (TOE-foo). Tofu has been called "meat without bones." Check it out sometime if you haven't already. There's probably no food on Earth that looks, tastes, or feels like tofu.

Another plant with complete protein is quinoa (KEEN-wa). It's an herb that looks like a grain and was a favorite of the ancient Incas in Mexico. It can be used in cereals, breads, and snack foods. Hey, why not invent "Quinoa Qubes" and become the first new billionaire snack-food tycoon of the twenty-first century?

Big hands.

If you're holding eight apples in one hand and nine oranges in the other hand, what do you have?

THE INSIDE SCOOP ON VITAMINS—
DON'T EVER, EVER FORGET US

There are thirteen little things you need to remember before your body can use protein, carbohydrates, and fats. Thirteen major vitamins, that is. All vitamins come from living things—plants and animals—and they help your body use other nutrients. If you had a perfect diet, with perfectly fresh food, you might get all the vitamins you need. But many people try to fill in the gaps by taking vitamin pills. It can be a good idea if your doctor approves.

It's important to remember that vitamins don't work alone. They work *with* the food you eat. Check out the following list, and you'll find some vitamins that work specially with carbohydrates, proteins, and/or fats to do amazing things in your body. That's why it's best to get your vitamins directly from the food you eat—the carbohydrates, proteins, and fats are built in. If you use vitamin pills, it's best to take them with a meal.

Fresh Facts About Vitamins

Which has more vitamins?

Though the tomato is a fruit—actually a berry—the U.S. Supreme Court ruled in 1893 that the tomato is a vegetable.

A big bag of raw green beans
that was picked last week

A big can of cooked green beans
that was picked last year

Get the can opener . . . If you lived in a perfect world on a perfect farm, things might be different. And not just because of the flying tractors. You'd be able to eat vegetables minutes after they were picked and get all the vitamins they provide.

But in the real world, many vegetables lose nearly half their vitamins within a few days of being harvested. By the time they reach your table, most of a vegetable's vitamins may have turned into carbohydrates.

Although cooking and canning also destroy some vitamins, the loss nearly stops once the vegetables are in the can. The best companies can their foods within hours after picking.

Absolutely fresh is best, but when you can't get foods fresh from the farm—or you're not sure about freshness—canned, frozen, or dried foods are just fine.

Cooking? Cleaning?

No, not those boring household chores that adults are always moaning about. Our question is this—does washing and cooking foods affect their nutrition? The answer is . . . sometimes. Some vitamins dissolve in water (water-soluble vitamins). Some dissolve in fats and oils (fat-soluble vitamins). Some are damaged by the heat of cooking. But losing a few vitamin molecules is better than eating the bacteria on a dirty mushroom or in a blob of raw hamburger. In fact, scientists have found that some vegetables provide better nutrition when they're cooked. Cook a carrot, for example, and the heat damages some of the vitamins. *But*, scientists say, the heat also breaks down some of the carrot's structure and releases more vitamins than you'd ever get from a raw carrot.

This'll Bowl You Over

An easy source of extra vitamins is the milk left at the bottom of your cereal bowl. Milk contains water and usually fat, so it easily dissolves both water- and fat-soluble vitamins. By the time you're done with your cereal, you've created your own secret vitamin potion at the bottom of your bowl. Go ahead. Slurp it up. Nobody's watching.

VITAMINS

Vitamin A, also called retinol, comes from egg yolks, carrots, leafy vegetables, and milk. It helps your cells grow and helps you see in low light. Fat soluble.

Vitamin B₁, also called thiamin, comes from pork, seafood, whole grains, sunflower seeds, peas, potatoes, nuts, and yogurt. It helps your body use carbohydrates, and it helps produce the stomach acid you need. Water soluble.

Vitamin B₂, also known as riboflavin, comes from milk, eggs, dark meat of poultry, whole grains, spinach, and cereals. It helps your body get energy from carbohydrates and proteins. Water soluble.

Vitamin B₃, also called niacin and nicotinic acid, comes from whole grains, poultry, fish, ham, peanuts, and peanut butter. It helps with digestion, helps convert food to energy, and helps keep your appetite normal. Water soluble.

Vitamin B₅, also called pantothenic acid, is found in almost all plant and animal foods. It's important for growth. Water soluble.

Vitamin B₆, also called pyridoxine, is found in meat, poultry, fish, whole-grain cereals, potatoes, watermelon, bananas, and prunes. It helps your body use amino acids and helps make red blood cells. Water soluble.

Vitamin B₁₂, also called cobalamin, is found only in animal foods, but it can also be made by your intestinal bacteria. It's needed to make new red blood cells and to help all cells function. Water soluble.

Biotin is found in eggs, milk, meats, vegetables, and nuts. It's also made by intestinal bacteria. It helps your body use glucose and fatty acids. Water soluble.

Squash!

What vegetable do you get when a rhinoceros walks through your garden?

Folic acid, also known as folate or folacin, is found in beans, dark green vegetables, nuts, oranges, and whole-wheat products. It helps in making red blood cells and in using protein. Water soluble.

Vitamin C, also known as ascorbic acid, is found in citrus fruits, tomatoes, strawberries, broccoli, and green peppers. It helps keep gums healthy and helps heal wounds. Water soluble.

Vitamin D is found in fish oils, milk, and egg yolks. You can also get all you need for a day by exposing your skin (your face and hands will do) to sunlight for fifteen or twenty minutes. It helps your body use calcium and phosphorus and helps maintain healthy bones. Fat soluble.

Vitamin E comes from vegetable oils, beans, eggs, wheat germ, sunflower seeds, peanut butter, sweet potatoes, and seafood. It helps prevent cell damage. Fat soluble.

Vitamin K is found in yogurt, leafy green vegetables, and egg yolks. It's also produced by intestinal bacteria. It helps your blood clot after an injury. Fat soluble.

THE INSIDE SCOOP ON MINERALS—
YES, YOU HAVE TO EAT THE CRUST

The Earth's crust, that is. There are ten to twenty minerals that should be in your chyme. You're sitting on top of them right now. These minerals are elements that were originally in the Earth's crust. Over millions of years, through volcanic explosions and other fun events, they found their way into the soil and water. Then into plants. And into animals that ate the plants. Now it's your turn.

Your body wouldn't work without minerals. Without potassium and sodium your brain couldn't flicker thoughts around, and your heart wouldn't beat. Without calcium you'd just be a blob without bones. Like vitamins, minerals work with food, so minerals are best when you get them directly from food as part of a meal. But people often try to cover their mineral needs by taking a pill. If your doctor agrees, taking a pill with a meal will work best.

Here's a list of fifteen minerals your body needs, where they come from, and some of what they do for you:

MINERALS

Calcium is one of the minerals your body needs in the greatest amount. Two of the best sources are milk and fish with bones soft enough to eat, like canned sardines and salmon. It's also found in leafy green vegetables. Calcium is the main material in your bones and teeth. It also helps regulate your heartbeat and move your muscles.

Chloride is found in table salt, fish, meat, milk, and eggs. It helps your body balance its water supply and blood chemistry. It also helps form stomach acid (it's the "chlori" in hydro*chlori*c).

Chromium is found in meat, cheese, whole grains, peas, and beans. It helps your body use glucose.

Copper comes from shellfish, nuts, meat, chocolate, beans, and raisins. It helps form red blood cells, is involved in helping the body use iron, and helps produce chemicals in the lungs.

Fluorine comes from fluoridated water, fish, tea, and gelatin desserts. It helps makes bones and teeth more solid. In the 1940s, scientists noticed something about communities where fluorine was found naturally in the drinking water—the people had less tooth decay. Since then, many communities with low levels of fluorine have added the mineral to their water supplies.

Iodine is found in iodized salt, seafood, seaweed, and dairy products. It helps your thyroid gland work, and it helps keep skin, hair, and nails healthy. It's not always easy to get enough naturally. In the 1920s, scientists suggested adding iodine to table salt to help prevent a common thyroid swelling called goiter.

Iron comes from red meats, egg yolks, peas, beans, nuts, dried fruits, and green vegetables like spinach. It helps the blood carry oxygen and is used in making enzymes and protein.

Magnesium is found in whole grains, raw leafy green vegetables, nuts, soybeans, bananas, and apricots. It helps your bones grow, your muscles work, and your heart beat.

What kind of jokes do vegetables like?
Corny ones.

Manganese is found in nuts, whole grains, vegetables, fruits, cocoa, and egg yolks. It helps bones grow and develop and helps cells function.

Molybdenum is found in peas, beans, grains, and dark green vegetables. It helps cells function.

Phosphorus is present in almost all foods. It's very important in bone growth, helps strengthen your teeth, and helps you use energy.

Potassium comes from oranges, bananas, dried fruits, peanuts, peas, beans, potatoes, yogurt, and meat. It helps keep your heartbeat regular, make your muscles move, carry nutrients to cells, and balance your body water.

Selenium comes from fish, shellfish, red meat, egg yolks, chicken, garlic, grains, and tomatoes. It works with vitamin E to prevent damage to cells.

Sodium comes from salt in foods, like canned products and processed foods. It helps balance water in your body's tissues and blood. It's easy to get too much.

Zinc is found in shellfish, beef, eggs, poultry, and whole wheat. It helps you taste and smell things, and it helps wounds heal.

Oh, Yes. And Don't Forget to Wash Down All Your Carbohydrates, Fats, Protein, Vitamins, and Minerals with Eight Cups of Water!

Water is so important it gets its own chapter!

Water Addiction:
Try Going Without It. Just Try.

The next time you see one of those huge chrome gasoline-tanker trucks pulling into your local Amoco or Exxon, imagine drinking the whole thing. Okay—if it were full of water. And yes, you can use two straws.

In your lifetime, you'll likely finish off one of these 9,000-gallon trucks by the time you're middle-aged. And then you'll go on to finish another. And start a third. A body will need 18,250 gallons of liquids just to keep itself running over an eighty-year lifetime. An average car, on the other hand, will only burn about 5,000 gallons of gasoline during its time on the road. Thirsty?

The fact is, you're always thirsty. You might think your blood is some special red fluid, but it's actually 82 percent water, transporting blood cells and nutrient molecules all over your body. At the same time, the water in your blood is always busy collecting your cells' waste—mostly nitrogen and excess salt molecules. Your body releases enough water to sweep this waste out of your body in urine, sweat, and breath. That's why an adult needs about two and a half quarts of clean replacement water every day.

Water is the only fluid your body actually uses. When you drink a milkshake, your body sees it only as various fat and protein molecules mixed up in water. A typical can of soda? Nine teaspoons of sugar molecules and a sprinkling of other chemicals mixed up in 12 ounces of water. Apples and oranges are like sweet fiber-and-vitamin sponges full of water. Your body even pulls water out of things like bread and cheese. Your intestines pull water out of everything you eat and drink.

If you don't get your 2.5 quarts of water a day from drinking and eating, your body suffers. Losing only 2 percent of your body's water can make you weak because the nitrogen and salts in your blood start crowding out the glucose and nutrients. A 5 percent loss causes exhaustion. A 7 to 15 percent loss is good news for your local flock of vultures.

How long can you go without water? Experts seem to agree it's about one week. But during those last few days you'd just be lying there hallucinating. That's when hula dancers and waterfalls begin making appearances in the desert.

Water Weight

Next time you're in the supermarket, gather together eight one-gallon jugs of water, line them up on the floor, and consider. That's about how much water is in the cells, body structures, and blood of a 100-pound person. Each gallon weighs 8.34 pounds, so the total is about 66 pounds! As you block traffic in the aisle, explain to angry shoppers that a person cannot mess with this level of water without messing up his or her body. Then put all those jugs back on the shelf before the store manager tosses you into the parking lot!

The Truth About Sweat

When someone says "no sweat," it's a lie. If you're alive, you're sweating. Most of it evaporates as soon as it reaches your skin surface, though. When your body really needs to cool down, your 2 million sweat glands pump excess hot water out of your blood. Next thing you know, you're thirsty.

Do You Squeak?

Put your hand near your ear. Wiggle your fingers and listen carefully. How about your eyeballs? Move them around and around really fast. Hear any squeaks? That's because water lubricates your joints and eyeballs, as well as your nasal passages and intestines.

The World's Most Unappealing Six-Pack

In a typical day you:

- Exhale enough water to fill about one soda can.
- Sweat enough water to fill about one and a half soda cans.
- Urinate enough water to fill about four soda cans.

Question: *Hey, what about the three cans of spit we produce every day?*

Answer: Most people swallow all their spit. (Note: This does not fully apply to professional baseball players during games.)

Don't Let a Camel Fool You . . .

Camels may think they're pretty slick walking around the desert with their humps and their reputation for not needing water for months. Well, here's the truth. Those humps are just fat, and a camel can go only about nine days without water—two days more than a human. So there!

Someday We'll Just Pop Nutrition Pills Instead of Eating, Right?

Back in the 1900s, comic books had some pretty wild ideas about life after 2000. Cars would fly. Everyone would have a robot butler. And we wouldn't have to eat—we'd just take nutrition pills.

Well, jeepers! (A little twentieth-century lingo there.) Did anybody know how many nutrition pills we'd have to take?

The protein in a typical day's food might weigh about 50 grams. That would be about 200 protein pills a day! (Pharmacists say the average pill weighs a quarter of a gram.)

And get a load of this—we need about 300 grams of carbohydrates. That would be about 1,200 carbohydrate pills a day!

Fats? No more than 65 grams a day, so add another 260 fat pills a day, max.

Ladies and gentlemen, we're talking close to 1,500 nutrition pills a day here. You'd have one very busy robot butler. . . .

The Large and Small of It

Proteins, carbohydrates, and fats are called macronutrients (maa-crow-NEW-tree-ents). You need large quantities of them. Vitamins and minerals are called micronutrients because you only need "micro" amounts—but that doesn't mean they're less important. It *is* possible to squeeze all your vitamins and minerals for a day into a single pill. It's best to get them from food, though, because vitamins, minerals, and food work together in our bodies.

How Much Is a Gram, Anyway?

A gram doesn't weigh much. It's easier to think about 5 grams at a time. A nickel coin weighs about 5 grams. Want to know how much your daily carbohydrates, protein, and fats might weigh? Stack up eighty-three nickels.

Eating in Orbit

You've been working hard in space all day, flipping switches, talking on the radio, and looking out the window. So out of which toothpaste tube would you like to squeeze your supper? That's the way it was in the early days of space flight. Flight planners tried to provide balanced meals with nutrition cubes, powders, and pastes. It didn't take long for hungry space cowboys to get cranky. Soon regular Earth food started finding its way onto space flights. Shrimp cocktail, steak, and chicken with vegetables are now common. Sometimes the food is ready to eat; sometimes it needs a little water. It's heated in an oven, and the astronauts eat with regular forks, knives, and spoons. The only things they have to worry about are crumbs. In space, crumbs float around and clog up the autogyrothingamajiggers.

Don't Tell Your School Cafeteria

How wild is your lunchroom? Imagine dining in a prison cafeteria. To discourage prisoners from hurling pieces of food across the room, prison officials in Oregon, Washington, Arizona, and Michigan experimented with a thing called Nutrition Loaf. They took a balanced assortment of meat, vegetables, rice, fruit, bread chunks, eggs, and more and ground it up into a paste. Then they baked it and served it to the prisoners in 10-ounce slabs. That was the whole meal. A newspaper reporter in Washington tasted it and called it unspeakably bad. A convicted murderer in Arizona sued his prison, saying food that bad violated his constitutional rights. He won.

Gopher Guts, Part 1
Great green globs of greasy, grimy gopher guts
Mutilated monkey meat
Little birdies' dirty feet
Great green globs of greasy, grimy gopher guts
And I forgot my spoon!

6 UNDERSTANDING A NUTRITION-FACTS LABEL

The Facts About Foodooz

Before 1992, people had no idea what to eat or how much to eat. Well, it wasn't quite that bad, but it *was* more confusing. Since 1992, we've had "Nutrition Facts" labels on our food packages.

These labels give you some clues about how foods compare and fit into your day's nutritional needs. What they're really trying to say is, "Here's the share of nutrients this product would provide for a person who eats about 2,000 calories worth of food a day."

There's nothing magic about this number. The government had to use *some* number as a starting point, and that's what they picked. As a growing kid, you probably need more than 2,000 calories—much more if you get lots of exercise.

The labels are really only a rough guide to help you compare the nutrients in similar products. To get an idea how to read Nutrition-Facts labels, compare the following labels for two brands of Foodooz, an imaginary breakfast item from the mythical Island of Highly Unusual Neighbors.

Which Foodooz Would You Chooz?

1. **Nutrition Facts**
   Serving Size One Foodoo (45g)
   Servings Per Container 10

2. **Amount Per Serving**
   Calories 100
   Calories from Fat 63

	% Daily Value*
Total Fat 7 g	**11%**
Saturated Fat 4 g	**20%**
Cholesterol 66 mg	**22%**
Sodium 360 mg	**15%**
Total Carbohydrate 5 g	**2%**
Dietary Fiber 0 g	**0%**
Sugars 5 g	
Protein 4 g	

Vitamin A 0%   **Vitamin C** 0%
Calcium 0%   **Iron** 1%

* Percent Daily Values are based on a 2,000 calorie diet. Your daily values may be higher or lower depending on your calorie needs.

		Calories:	2,000	2,500
Total Fat	Less than		65 g	80 g
Sat Fat	Less than		20 g	25 g
Cholesterol	Less than		300 mg	300 mg
Sodium	Less than		2,400 mg	2,400 mg
Total Carbohydrate			300 g	375 g
Dietary Fiber			25 g	30 g

Calories per gram:
Fat 9 • Carbohydrate 4 • Protein 4

(The numbers **1.** through **10.** appear as callouts pointing to sections of the Nutrition Facts label.)

1. Just an idea of **serving size**. If you're comparing products, make sure the serving sizes are about the same. (See page 47.)

2. For a whole day, less than 30 percent* (30 in 100) of your **calories** should come from fat. Zoodoof Brand can help you keep to that level.

3. For **total fat**, **saturated fat**, **cholesterol**, and **sodium**, lower percents are better. If you see anything above 20 percent in this section, that's not good. If the saturated-fat listing includes asterisks, that means the product also contains trans fats. Zoodoof Brand wins again.

4. If grams of **total carbohydrate** are more than double the grams of **sugars**, that's good. It means the product is high in complex carbohydrates—the kind you want for steady energy. Go with the Zoodoof.

For all you math whizzes . . . To figure out 30 percent of any number, just multiply the number by 30 and then divide the answer by 100.

Nutrition Facts
Serving Size One Foodoo (45g)
Servings Per Container 10

Amount Per Serving

Calories 100
Calories from Fat 27

	% Daily Value*
Total Fat 3 g	**5**%
Saturated Fat 1 g	**5**%
Cholesterol 18 mg	**6**%
Sodium 370 mg	**15**%
Total Carbohydrate 14 g	**5**%
Dietary Fiber 1 g	**4**%
Sugars 2 g	
Protein 4 g	

Vitamin A 2%		**Vitamin C** 5%	
Calcium 2%		**Iron** 0%	

* Percent Daily Values are based on a 2,000 calorie diet. Your daily values may be higher or lower depending on your calorie needs.

		Calories:	2,000	2,500
Total Fat	Less than		65 g	80 g
Sat Fat	Less than		20 g	25 g
Cholesterol	Less than		300 mg	300 mg
Sodium	Less than		2,400 mg	2,400 mg
Total Carbohydrate			300 g	375 g
Dietary Fiber			25 g	30 g

Calories per gram:
Fat 9 • Carbohydrate 4 • Protein 4

1.
2.
3.
4.
5.
6.
7.
8.
9.
10.

5. Any grams of **dietary fiber** are good. Zoodoof Brand wins yet again.

6. In general, anything above 9 or 10 grams of **protein** means this is a high-protein food. It's a tie.

7. If any of the numbers for **vitamins** and **minerals** are above 10, that's good. If any are above 20, that's great. Zoodoof Brand? It's not great, but better than El Presidente.

8. Just general information. It explains that the percentage numbers listed above are based on a 2,000 calorie diet.

9. More general information. Because few people hit 2,000 calories on the nose, this shows how recommended levels compare for diets with 2,000 calories and 2,500 calories.

10. Just a reminder that a gram of fat always gives you 9 calories, and carbohydrates and proteins always give you 4 calories per gram.

Okay, Let's Total It Up

Like a lot of foods, El Presidente Foodooz are sweet (sugars are more than half the total carbohydrates), fatty (high in saturated fat), and salty (more than 20 percent of all your sodium for the day). And they don't give you much good stuff. Sometimes prestige is a funny thing.

Zoodoof Brand Foodooz seem to be somewhat worthwhile. Total carbohydrates are more than twice the sugars, so you'll be getting some steady energy. Zoodoof also gives you some fiber and some vitamins and minerals. Hey, without all that prestige, Zoodoof Brand is probably cheaper, too.

Foodooz Are Made from WHAT!?!

Like all foods in packages, boxes of Foodooz would include a printed ingredients list. This helps you find out what's really in there. The ingredients are listed in order of their weight in the product. The heaviest ingredient in the product goes first, the second heaviest goes second, and so on. If a product has extra good stuff in it—like vitamins or minerals—the company usually puts that on the label, too.

Gopher Guts, Part 2
Great green globs of greasy, grimy gopher guts
Mutilated monkey meat
Marinated weasel feet
French-fried eyeballs rolling down a muddy street
And I forgot my spoon!

A NEW ANGLE ON THE FOOD-GUIDE PYRAMID

The Right Way to Eat

By now everyone's seen the government's Food-Guide Pyramid. It gives you good ideas about choosing your everyday food— what kind of foods you should eat and how much of everything. It's a good guide, but here's a question. . . . What does a *pyramid* have to do with *food*? A pyramid is a huge stone thing full of shriveled-up pharaohs in the middle of the desert. *Not appetizing!*

And so, without further ado, we turn the nutrition world upside down and introduce, for the first time anywhere, the fabulous, the fantastic, the not-so far-fetched . . .

FOOD *RULES!* Food Funnel!!!!!!!

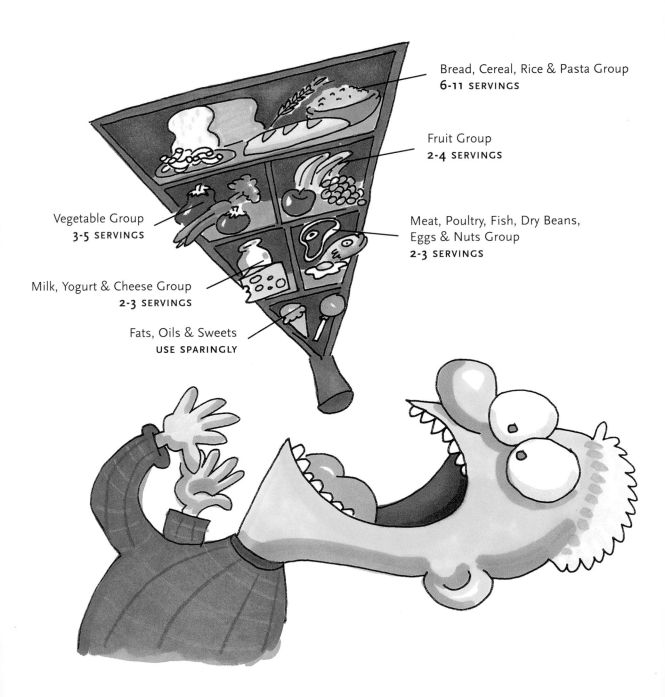

Bread, Cereal, Rice & Pasta Group
6-11 SERVINGS

Fruit Group
2-4 SERVINGS

Vegetable Group
3-5 SERVINGS

Meat, Poultry, Fish, Dry Beans, Eggs & Nuts Group
2-3 SERVINGS

Milk, Yogurt & Cheese Group
2-3 SERVINGS

Fats, Oils & Sweets
USE SPARINGLY

What's a Serving, Anyway?

Food guidelines mention two daily servings of this and three servings of that, but what's a serving? A whole cabbage? One brussels sprout? Though the guidelines vary as much as the food itself, here are some easy-to-remember facts about serving sizes:

* One serving of meat is about the size of a deck of playing cards. Same with fish and tofu.
* Fruits like apples, oranges, or a bunch of grapes should be about the size of a tennis ball to qualify as a serving.
* A slice of bread or half of a bagel is one serving. Make a sandwich, and you have two bread-group servings right there. In this same group, a scoop of spaghetti or blob of rice about the size of a computer mouse is considered one serving.
* The amount of most vegetables in a serving depends on whether they're cooked or raw. Cooked? A serving equals about one-half cup of vegetables. Raw? About one cup.
* For dairy products, figure on a cup of milk as one serving or about two slices of cheese.
* It's easy to eat too much from the fat, oils, and sweets group. There are no serving sizes recommended because the rule is simple—the less you eat from this group, the better.

Some Extra Nutritional Advice, Courtesy of _Food Rules!_

Never eat anything bigger than your head.

The United Nations reported in the 1970s that the biggest sources of meat in West Africa were rats and mice. In Thailand, they say rats taste like rabbit—better than chicken.

8 WHAT'S MALNUTRITION?

A Good Diet Is Beriberi Important

The word *malnutrition* brings to mind starving children in poor countries. But the fact is, malnutrition just means bad nutrition, and it can happen to anyone. Picky eaters. Kids going through growth spurts. People who try to change their bodies by changing the amount or type of food they eat. People who change their diets to support a cause. No matter what, it's never good to forget about vitamins and minerals and the basic guidelines shown in the <u>Food *Rules!*</u> Food Funnel.

Pirates didn't know that going to sea for months without vitamin C from fruit could cause a disease called scurvy and make their teeth fall out. And you thought it was just because pirates didn't brush.

A hundred years ago, a disease called beriberi was found wherever people tried to live only on milled rice. Beriberi caused problems in the nerves, brain, and heart. It took a while to figure out that milling removed something in the rice that prevented these problems. It took even longer to realize the "something" was simply vitamin B_1.

Some people try to cut calories and unknowingly cut nutrients they need. They can wind up skinny and sick. Other people eat too many "empty-calorie" foods with lots of calories but not much else. They can wind up fat and sick.

Now some people are just naturally fat or skinny, healthy or unhealthy, and food doesn't have much to do with it. But for most people, knowing and remembering a bit about vitamins, minerals, carbohydrates, fats, protein, and water is a big step toward feeling good and staying healthy.

Sit in the Dark Without Milk

That's the way to get a bone disease called rickets. It's caused by a lack of vitamin D—the only vitamin you can get from both nutrition and sunlight. Milk is an excellent source of it. Rickets was once common in cities during the winter. Without nearby farms, milk was scarce, and the cold weather and short days kept people inside and away from any sunlight. Rickets can slow down a child's growth and cause bones to soften at any age.

To many people in Asia, the thought of drinking a cow's milk is disgusting. So how about fermented dried-up cow's milk (cheese)? Out of the question!

Your Hungry Heart

When you lose or gain a lot of weight, there are changes in the weight of your heart, liver, kidneys, intestines, and other organs, too. That's why it's a bad idea to go on a serious diet without telling a doctor what you have in mind. Want to lose or gain weight? A doctor can help you do it without damage. Looking in a mirror doesn't tell you what's going on inside.

Don't Waste Your Taste

Eating is actually a lot of work. Teeth grinding, tongue pushing, throat squeezing. Then there's digestion, not to mention a table to clean up. Growth and energy are great, but there must be some other reward. Something exciting. Something instant. It's called taste.

Imagine shoveling coal into a train's engine. It's a lot of work, too. But what if, with every shovelful, you got a little tickle and a memory of something nice. That's kind of how taste works. It uses tickles and memories to keep you shoveling.

The whole thing starts with smell. Just a whiff of pepperoni pizza can start the saliva flowing and tell your whole digestive system that something's coming. You get the tickle from the taste buds on your tongue. They check out the chemicals in the food. Are the chemicals sweet? Sour? Salty? Bitter? Four types of taste buds pepper your brain with messages about these four tastes.

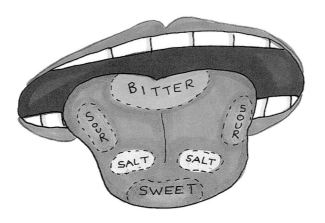

America, with amber waves of grain and purple mountain majesties and so forth, was found because Europeans wanted an easier way to get spices from Asia to make their food taste better.

Whole roast dog is a traditional favorite in Hawaii and Samoa. A voyager to Hawaii said it tastes like lamb.

But using only your tongue to taste food is like watching black-and-white TV. It's your sense of smell as you chew that really brings you the full flavor of food. Your brain receives messages about smell in the same area that stores memories and emotions. That may be why people so often use the words *love* and *hate* when talking about food. They really do *love* chocolate and *hate* anchovies.

Just like your emotions, your tastes for food can change. People you didn't like last year are probably now your friends. It's the same with food. You'll be amazed when some of the foods you can't stand today become your favorites. Discovering that you like new foods is one of the really nice things about growing up. But just as with people, the only way to find out is to give them a chance.

Your Tongue Is Not a Toy

But that doesn't mean you can't play with it. Some of the most fun you can have with a candy cane is checking out your taste buds. Open your mouth wide, stick out your tongue, and hold your nose with one hand. With your other hand, touch the end of a candy cane to the rear area of your tongue and nowhere else. Can you really taste it? How about if you touch it along the middle and the sides of your tongue? How about if you touch it to the *tip* of your tongue? Aha! But . . . does it *really* taste like a candy cane or just taste sweet? Okay, let go of your nose. *How about now?!!!* By the way, don't do this with anything you can choke on. A candy cane is a good choice because it has a built-in safety retrieval handle.

Oooh Mommy, It's Umami

The four basic tastes—sweet, sour, bitter, and salty—may be joined by a fifth. In Japan, cooks have long talked about a totally separate taste called umami. The idea seems to be catching on around the world. Umami has been described as the hard-to-explain flavor that's in mushrooms and Parmesan cheese.

The 1999 Hot-Dog Eating Contest winner was a 317-pound electrical inspector who ate 20¼ franks and buns in twelve minutes.

What makes some foods crunchy? Tiny explosions! When you bite a potato chip or stalk of celery, you're popping open hundreds of tiny cells of air. It's like stomping on a sheet of bubble wrap—who can resist? In some foods, like apples, the cells are filled with water, but the crunch is just as much fun.

Give Yourself a Food Mustache

Can different smells change the taste of food? Well, here's an experiment that lets you smear food on your face and get away with it *in the name of science*! The idea is to smear smelly food under your nose and notice what it does to the flavor of things you eat. Try a ketchup mustache and eat some chocolate. Try a chocolate-syrup mustache and eat a hot dog. What does a mustard mustache do to tofu? Now, don't smear so much that you inhale your mustache. Remember, these are supposed to be *tasteful* mustaches.

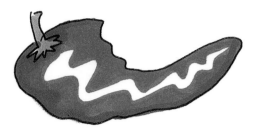

If It's "Chilly," Then Why Is It So *Hot*?

There are legends about the amazing heat of hot chili peppers. Cartoon characters take a bite, and their heads explode. In Costa Rica, chili pepper pickers picking pecks of chili peppers have to dress like astronauts to avoid blisters. Are chili peppers really hot in temperature? The answer is *no*! Even the Red Savina Habanero—the hottest chili pepper in the world—wouldn't raise the temperature of your tongue, but it might cause a blister. The "heat" you think you feel comes from a chemical in chili peppers called capsaicin (cap-SAY-sin). When it touches your skin, especially sensitive skin, capsaicin opens pain pathways to your brain—the same pathways that open when you stick your foot in a too-hot bath. Your brain thinks it feels heat. Too much capsaicin can injure skin cells and break down these pain pathways. That's why peppers don't seem to bother people who eat a lot of them. They can't feel them anymore! But never fear, the cells and pathways seem to grow back eventually.

Tasting Something Bad Can Be Good

Our senses of taste and smell also protect us from food that's gone bad. Crack open a rotten egg, and people across the room will know it. And *nobody's* going to eat it. Food gets that "off" smell and taste when bacteria or fungi have been feeding. Having no manners, the bacteria and fungi dump their waste right where they eat, giving off a sulfury smell and taste. We're programmed to say "yeeeech!!!" when we smell it because eating spoiled food can make us sick. Exceedingly bitter-tasting food can also signal possible problems—like the presence of poison.

Big on Taste

Consider the chicken. Day after day it eats the same thing. Grain. No wonder a chicken needs only 45 taste buds. Dogs? They're made to like meat, all kinds. Dogs have about 2,000 taste buds. Humans eat grain, vegetables, fruit, meat, fish, even pizza, yogurt, and cafeteria food. We have about 10,000 taste buds. Now think of a catfish, snooping along the bottom of a creek. A catfish has an astounding 100,000 taste buds, some even on its body, enabling it to enjoy just about anything that falls into the water. Yum!

Quiz for Extra Credit

Q: How many taste buds does a unicorn have?

A: None. There's no such thing as a unicorn.

During a beef shortage in 1973, American newspapers reported great interest in "horse meat butcher shops" in Connecticut and Washington. Donkey meat is said to be even more flavorful than horse meat.

What Do You Mean You Can't Go?

So you've destroyed an entire bag of Cavity Crunch Snack Dingers. You turned them all into green slimy chyme and sent the chyme oozing through your small intestine. The Cavity Crunch's fat and sugar molecules are now whizzing around in your bloodstream. (Yow! Check the Nutrition-Facts label on the package to see how much.) Now what happens? Well, check that Cavity Crunch label again and see if it lists *fiber*.

Fiber is simply the stuff that your stomach and small intestine can't completely break down into molecules. It's kind of like sawdust, and it never gets small enough to sneak through your intestinal wall and into your bloodstream. You get fiber from the woody parts of fruits, vegetables, beans, and grains—the skins and structure.

Fiber stays in the chyme as it flows from your hungry small intestine into your thirsty large intestine. The large intestine soaks up extra water in the chyme and sends the water molecules into your bloodstream. As the chyme gives up its water, it gets thicker and thicker. By the time it reaches the end of the large intestine, it's no longer like slimy pea soup. It's thick and chunky and looks kind of like clay. But it's not clay. It's poop! Or, as scientists and polite people at polo matches call it, feces (FEE-seas).

Fiber-packed feces are happy feces. They're soft and bulky, and they're ready to come out. Imagine clay with sawdust mashed all through it. Without fiber, feces are more like just plain clay. The pieces are smaller, drier, and harder. They tend to hang around for a long time. Your body stores lots of them before unloading. Storing hard, dry feces in your body is not a good idea. They're hard to squeeze out. They can even make you grumpy, and you won't know why.

Not everything you eat will have fiber. In fact, almost no animal-based foods do. All your fiber has to come from plant-based foods. But . . . plant fiber is often lost when foods go through processing. For example, sugar has no fiber. White flour has very little. Some companies *add* fiber to their processed foods or make a special effort to leave it in. So check your labels. If Cavity Crunch doesn't list much fiber, make sure you also eat stuff during the day that does. Like popcorn.

Pop Your Way to Bathroom Bliss

For fiber, plain, air-popped popcorn is one of the best things you can snack on. One serving of popcorn gives you six times more fiber than one serving of most potato chips. That's because popcorn gives you the whole kernel— it's a whole food. Most potato chips are processed—they're peeled, which removes a lot of the fiber that was in the skin. Make your snacks do some work for you. Go with the popcorn!

Fiber Up

Humans should eat between 20 and 35 grams of fiber a day. Most American humans eat only about 13 grams. Want to make the grade? It's not that hard. Here's a good day's worth of fiber:

Four slices of whole-wheat bread	8 grams
Two apples	5 grams
Big bowl of popcorn	6 grams
Two carrots	3 grams

Why Brown?

You eat a red apple and a blue ice pop, trying to create purple poop. But every day it's the same old thing. Brown, brown, brown. Why? Well, stomach acid destroys most of your food's color as soon as you swallow it. Then a fat-digesting chemical called bile makes everything greenish-brownish in your small intestine. Then bacteria in your intestines turns the greenish color to brown. Plus, your body gets rid of old, dead, brown blood cells by mixing them up in there. Tired of brown? Flush!

The Proof Is in the Corn

Every once in a while feces appear decorated by corn kernels. That's just proof that fiber doesn't get digested. A kernel of corn is completely surrounded by a layer of fiber. If your teeth don't happen to puncture that layer, the kernel goes all the way through your digestive system intact. Everything stays inside the kernel, including the nutrients and the yellow color. Want to avoid the corn surprise? Puncture every corn kernel with your teeth. Chew! Be sure to interrupt anyone wolfing down a hot, buttered ear of corn and explain this. It makes for delightful picnic conversation.

FOOD-RELATED ILLNESSES

This Stuff Makes Me Sick

Kills thousands of germs on contact! No, we're not talking about some amazing household spray. We're talking about the hydrochloric acid in your stomach. One of its jobs is to help make sure the food you eat doesn't have live harmful bacteria or viruses in it. How? It gives the invaders an acid bath. It dissolves them. And it does a good job. But every once in a while—especially if you eat something with a lot of the wrong kind of bacteria or viruses in it—some of it slips through your stomach and into your small intestine. In there it's like a germ paradise—all kinds of nutrients at just the right temperature. The bad bacteria make more bacteria, which make more bacteria, which make more bacteria, and soon your brain says, "Get that stuff out of there!"

Your intestines then quickly squeeze the chyme along without bothering to absorb the nutrients and water. The result is often loose, watery poop called diarrhea (die-ah-REE-ah). All this squeezing is sometimes called a bellyache. Diarrhea and bellyaches can also be caused by poisons, food allergies, or your stomach making too much acid.

Sometimes the bacteria, viruses, or poisons get only as far as your stomach when your brain says "out!" Your stomach squeezes hard and you throw up.

How can you outsmart food bacteria? Well, bacteria are everywhere, and there's no way to avoid *all* the bacteria that's in your food. In fact, some bacteria—like the type found in yogurt—is good for you. It's used in digestion. What you want to do is keep the numbers of harmful bacteria as low as possible. This gives your stomach acid a better chance to kill 'em all. How do you keep the numbers low? All the simple things you've always heard about:

1. Before you touch or cook food, wash your hands.
2. Always wash your hands before you eat.
3. If you touch raw meat or fish, wash your hands.
4. Keep cold foods cold, hot foods hot, and don't eat food that's been lying around at room temperature. Throw it out and then wash your hands.
5. Smell food before you eat it. If it doesn't smell right, don't eat it. If the food happened to touch your nose when you smelled it, wash your nose. Then wash your hands.
6. Keep flies off your food. Shoo them away before they land, and then wash your hands.
7. If you're making food, make sure it's cooked all the way through. See #1.

Do you see a pattern here?

People have great suspicions about hot-dog ingredients, but the truth is the U.S. Department of Agriculture requires that hot dogs must use muscle meat—not ground-up waste products. If things like hearts and livers are used, the ingredients must list "variety meats" or "meat by-products."

Shoo Fly, Don't Bother Me, Huh?

Insects aren't always dirty, but the common housefly is filthy. It lands and snacks on bacteria-covered rotting things, and then carries the bacteria to wherever it lands—like onto food. To spread the word about flies and food, a British health group once tried to get people disgusted about flies by putting up disgusting posters. The words said it all: "Flies can't eat solid food, so to soften it up, they vomit on it. Then they stomp the vomit in until it's liquid, usually stomping in some germs for good measure. Then when it's good and runny, they suck it all back again, and probably drop some excrement at the same time. And then . . . when they've finished eating . . . it's your turn."

Tapeworm Terror

Parasites live off other living creatures, and they're everywhere—even in our food. Sometimes they're microscopic, sometimes they're large enough to see. Cooking and stomach acid kills most of them, but every once in a while, you hear tales of terror involving tapeworms. Humans are most likely to get tapeworms from eating undercooked meat or fish. Tough, tiny tapeworm eggs in food sneak into the small intestine where they can hatch. Because tapeworms have no digestive system, they love to attach themselves inside the intestines and feed on the nutrients meant for the person. The person may lose weight, have diarrhea, or have no symptoms at all. A tapeworm can live inside a person for twenty-five years and never be noticed. Sometimes they break apart and are pooped out before they get too large, but a tapeworm can easily grow to thirty feet long or more. The largest one found in a human was said to be a whopping sixty-six feet long. Now don't freak out. It's usually easy for a doctor to find and treat a tapeworm problem. In fact, just one pill can kill it.

Zit True About Food Causing Pimples and Allergies?

Zits are no fun. But at least you can still eat chocolate and potato chips. Scientists say that eating has little, if any, effect on pimples. Teenagers just naturally produce more oil in their skin, and this leads to zits no matter what they eat.

Allergies to certain foods can be even less fun than zits. They can cause itching, rashes, swollen body parts, and breathing problems. Common food allergies include eggs, fish, cow's milk, peanuts, soybeans, and peaches. When you're allergic to a certain food, your body mistakes the food for an invading force. It fights back by releasing chemicals that can irritate your body and cause a bad reaction.

Some foods like peanuts can cause especially bad problems. Just being near peanuts can affect some people. Some airlines offer "peanut-free seating sections" so sensitive people won't have to sit where peanuts are served.

Food intolerance usually means your body doesn't have the ability to digest a particular food, like milk. Eating or drinking these foods can send you flying to the bathroom—or itching like a chimpanzee.

Peanuts aren't really nuts. They're beans.

Waiter You Hear These!

Guaranteed: The Ten Most Disgusting "Fly in Soup" Jokes in the World

Waiter, there's a fly in my soup!
Don't worry, ma'am, the spiders will get him.

Waiter, there's a fly in my soup!
Don't mention it, sir. No extra charge.

Waiter, what's this fly doing in my soup?
The backstroke, I think.

Waiter, there's a fly in my soup!
Shhh! Everyone will want one. . . .

Waiter, there's a fly in my soup!
Sorry, sir, I thought I'd scooped them all out.

Waiter, there's a dead fly in my soup!
Sorry, they're not very good swimmers.

Waiter, there's a fly in my soup!
Couldn't be, sir. The cook used them all in the raisin bread.

Waiter, there's a dead fly in my soup!
Sorry, ma'am. The poor little things just can't take the hot water.

Waiter, there's a mosquito in my soup.
Yes, sir. That's because we've run out of flies.

Waiter, there's a fly in my soup!
That's all right, ma'am, they don't drink much.

Onions, Garlic, Beans, and Your Popularity

"**H**ey, sulfur breath!" That, ladies and gentlemen, is the accurate way to complain when someone's breath is stinking up your air.

Most of us have bad breath once in a while, and almost all of it is caused by sulfur gases—the same type of gases that make a rotten egg one of the stinkiest things on Earth.

When you forget to brush and floss enough, food particles can hang around between your teeth and under your gums—sometimes for days. This makes a great meal for mouth bacteria. And when mouth bacteria eat, they fart sulfur gases. It's true! Most bad breath is really the germs' farts!

As if that's not enough, some foods *release* sulfur gases into your mouth as you *chew*! Garlic and onions, for example. After you swallow, garlic puts sulfur-containing molecules into your bloodstream. Many

Rats With Strong Bones, Even Stronger Breath: Swiss scientists found that rats fed dried onions for four weeks grew stronger, thicker bones than rats whose diets were onion-free.

scientists believe this is what helps make garlic a healthful food. *But* . . . the sulfur actually makes your blood stink! That's why people can sometimes tell you ate garlic even if you brush like crazy. They can smell it in your sweat and in the air that comes out of your lungs.

Burping and belching are far less complicated. It's simply the sound of air released from your stomach. There's always a little air in there, and some foods and drinks (carbonated ones, especially!) add even more air. Plus stomach acid breaking down food creates gas. When the pressure gets too great, a bubble of air slips out of your stomach and travels up and out of your mouth. A burp often smells and tastes like whatever you just ate. So you get to enjoy it twice.

And that brings us to the air that comes out of your other end. You know . . . when you cough in your pants. When you sit on a duck. Yes, you can blame your own farts on sulfur gas, too. (The official name for farting is *flatulence*—flat-CHOO-lents.) This time bacteria are chowing on the remaining food and fiber that's traveling through your large intestine. Fiber from beans provides a particularly enjoyable meal for bacteria, and that's why beans are sometimes called "the musical fruit." (Not that beans are fruit . . . Although the fiber in fruit can also cause a toot!)

The FOOD *RULES!* Poetry Competition

Two versions of an absolute classic, presented together for the first time. Why not gather your friends for a poetry reading? You can serve crumpets and bean dip and discuss which version you like better:

Beans, beans, good for your heart	*Beans, beans, the musical fruit*
The more you eat, the more you fart.	*The more you eat, the more you toot.*
The more you fart, the better you feel	*The more you toot, the better you feel*
So eat your beans at every meal!	*So eat your beans at every meal!*

Stopping Gas Before It Starts

Science and technology have changed our world in so many, many wonderful ways. But near the top of the <u>Food Rules!</u> list of scientific achievements is the development of oral alpha-galactosidase (al-fah-ga-lack-TOSS-ih-daze). Found in drugstores as "Beano" pills and liquid drops, this miracle enzyme is taken with meals and helps humans digest plant parts like bean skins and broccoli fiber. Digesting this kind of stuff leaves less for those obnoxious gas-producing bacteria to munch on. Results? Less gas, greater popularity. To learn more about the worldwide crusade for gas prevention, just pester your librarian for the November, 1994, issue of the *Journal of Family Practice*, and an article entitled "Does Beano Prevent Gas? A Double-Blind Crossover Study of Oral Alpha-Galactosidase to Treat Dietary Oligosaccharide Intolerance."

And When You Just Can't Help It...

We all know that gas prevention is only half the battle. What about those times when there's. . .well, a sneak attack? Technology to the rescue again, this time with the Toot Trapper, the first air filter disguised as an ordinary seat cushion. The company says it uses military gas-mask technology to "eliminate the human gas odor in your home, office, or car." Why not buy a set for the whole family?

The Sports Banquet: Can Food Make You Win?

Athletes' ideas about food are as varied as their shoes. Michael Jordan of the Chicago Bulls loved steak and eggs before every game. Triathlon champion Simon Lessing says he never eats before a race. In baseball, Greg Maddux of the Atlanta Braves says he likes a pre-game meal from Burger King or McDonald's. So who's right?

Maybe it's high-school marathon runners from South Korea. They follow this eight-day diet before every race:

> **First three days:** Beef and boiled eggs at every meal. No rice, no vegetables.
> **Second three days:** Vegetables, abalone porridge, walnuts, and pine nuts. No beef.
> **Day before the race:** Whipped-cream cake, a little rice, sour kimchi (fermented cabbage), seaweed, and anchovies.
> **Day of the race:** rice and water.

Meanwhile in the United States, runners prepare for the Boston Marathon by attending a huge pasta party the night before the race. At one recent party, 10,000 runners consumed lasagna, orzo, and gemelli made from 3,000 pounds of pasta and 2,000 quarts of tomato sauce.

Kenyans train for marathons by eating what is basically the national dish of Kenya: a cornmeal mush called ugali. Sometimes after running, they pass around huge platters of steaming hot lamb and a real delicacy made from goat intestines. Hey, don't knock it. In one Boston Marathon, Kenyans took the first five places.

So what's the right sports diet? It's hard to say. All sports require energy, and one way or another, your energy comes from glucose. All during a sporting event, your muscles tap into the glucose that's always whizzing around in your blood. The supply is constantly replaced by the glucose stored as glycogen in your muscles and liver. During exercise, your body can also tap into your fat and protein, which can convert to glucose if you need it.

These days, sports nutritionists say the key to an athlete's energy is the glucose stored as glycogen in the muscles and liver. You build and maintain this supply by eating carbohydrates over a long period of time. Stuffing yourself full of carbs the night before an event won't really help. You also need stores of protein and fat to help build and repair your muscle cells.

So maybe the Kenyans have it right. A steady diet of cornmeal mush carbohydrates plus an occasional goat-intestine protein and fats party. (Hey, doesn't that sound kind of like cornflakes and hot dogs?)

The Beauty of an Empty Stomach

It's actually a good thing, many sports nutrition experts agree, to compete on a stomach that's empty—and a small intestine that's full. Food that's still in your stomach and not digested won't help you during the game, and it can actually cause stomach cramps when you start bouncing around. The trick is having high-quality chyme in your small intestine. Most athletes find it's best to eat one to two hours before game time. That way, the food has left your stomach, and its molecules are filtering busily from your small intestine into your bloodstream.

Tripe is the stomach tissue of a cow, sheep, or ox.

Burning Energy

The energy your body uses and stores is measured in calories. Accurately counting the calories used in exercise is difficult because the amount depends on how much you weigh and how much your body needs just to stay alive (to keep your heart, lungs, brain, digestion, and everything else running). To get a general idea of energy used during exercise, let's look at the calories a 100-pound person might burn in some activities:

SLEEPING
1/2 calorie per minute

READING THIS BOOK
1 calorie per minute

PLAYING SOCCER
5 1/2 calories per minute

SWIMMING LAPS
8 calories per minute

**READING THIS BOOK
WHILE PLAYING SOCCER**
not advisable

ICE SKATING
5 1/2 calories per minute

PLAYING BASKETBALL
6 1/2 calories per minute

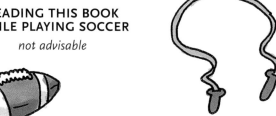

PLAYING TOUCH FOOTBALL
6 1/2 calories per minute

JUMPING ROPE
8 calories per minute

Chiefly Carbs

Every year the Kansas City Chiefs want to kick the tar out of every team in the NFL so they can win big, clunky Super Bowl rings. Their plan? Feed the team a mix of food that's 55 percent carbohydrate, no more than 30 percent fat, and 15 percent protein. Here's what the Chiefs serve every day in training camp:

Breakfast Thirteen main courses including grits, waffles, and creamed ham. Seven varieties of cereal. Six varieties of sweet rolls and dough-nuts. Ten different fruits.

Lunch Two main courses with side dishes. Deli bar, salad bar, fruit bar, pasta bar, and dessert bar.

Dinner Three main courses such as chicken Dijon, carved pork, and Cajun catfish. Deli bar, salad bar, fruit bar, pasta bar, and dessert bar.

Snack Pizza, bread sticks, garlic bread, hamburgers with everything, Chinese food, and Mexican food.

Too Busy Eating to Worry About the Game

Women's National Team soccer star Mia Hamm says she eats about five small meals in the hours before a game—things like cereal and fruit, a turkey or peanut-butter sandwich, some pasta, vegetables, and more fruit.

Heavy Competition

Like sports? Like to eat? Like to nap? Be a sumo wrestler! Sumo is the sport where two immense athletes—sometimes weighing as much as 600 pounds—heave their humongous bodies at each other, trying to knock each other down or out of a twelve-foot circle. It's wildly popular in Japan. Professional sumo wrestlers are recruited at about fifteen to nineteen years of age. They get up at six A.M., don't eat breakfast, and train for about five hours. Then they thunder into the lunchroom for their first meal of the day—a high-calorie stew called Chanko-nabe, which can include chicken, cabbage, fish, tofu, and many other ingredients. Side dishes include fried chicken, steak, salad, omelets, and endless bowls of rice. Eating twenty pounds of meat in one day is not uncommon. When they can no longer shovel food, the sumo wrestlers waddle off to their rooms to take nice afternoon naps, which is considered part of the training. Wonder what they dream about, those sumo wrestlers.

Turtles and Speed?
Newspapers reported that one of China's leading runners trains on a diet of worms, a tonic made from caterpillar fungus, and soup made from the blood of soft-shell turtles. C'mon now. It all turns into molecules, remember?

The Next Wave

New sports are always evolving, and so will new pre-game meal ideas. One player for the Sun Dried Yams, an Alabama Frisbee Team, enjoys macaroni and cheese with bananas before each Frisbee match.

Banana Abuse

Why did the banana go to the doctor?
Because it wasn't peeling well!

Have you heard about the new shoes made from banana peels?
They're called slippers.

What did the banana do when the monkey chased it?
The banana split.

WHAT'S SO GOOD ABOUT SEAFOOD?

Brain Food and Other Tales from the Deep

Does eating fish make you smarter? Does eating carrots make you see better? If you eat fish sticks and carrot sticks together, can you suddenly play chess in the dark?

Now *there's* an experiment. But seriously, scientists are now finding out that many of your grandparents' pronouncements about food are correct. (Meanwhile, in a laboratory across town, other scientists are finding out that your uncle George is wrong about nearly everything.)

So how about the "fish is brain food" idea? Well, scientists offer two reasons why it might be true: First, fish is a good source of DHA, the omega-3 fatty acid that is the building block of the brain. Second, fish contains vitamins like choline and fatty acids, which help messages move through the brain. Gee. Who wouldn't want a well-built brain that's really good at moving messages around?

What do whales eat?
Fish and ships.

74

Now, none of this happens overnight, and it's really just chemicals, not fishy magic. Once the vitamins and fatty acids are in your bloodstream, your body doesn't know or care that they came from fish. It's just that fish happens to be a very good source of these particular chemicals.

In fact, fish is a good source of all kinds of great things. Omega-3 fatty acids have also been linked to healthier hearts. And the protein in fish provides a good and complete balance of amino acids.

Still, the average American eats only about 18 pounds of fish per year, compared to 160 pounds of beef, pork, and poultry. But the amount of fish we eat is increasing. "Fish farms" are popping up everywhere—even in water tanks in the middle of cities. An up-and-coming farm fish was apparently an ancient favorite, too. Some historians believe that Bible stories mentioning fish were probably referring to tilapia (til-LOP-ee-ah), a football-shaped species common in the Nile River region.

Today, scientists say tilapia may be the most efficient form of livestock on Earth—fifty times less expensive to produce than beef, thirty-five times cheaper than chicken, and even four times cheaper than soybeans. To produce one pound of beef, a cow must eat sixteen pounds of grain. Producing one pound of tilapia meat only requires two pounds of grain. You don't need to eat fish to understand how smart fish farming is.

Tilapia Good; Fugu Bad

Meet fugu, the popular, poisonous puffer fish of Japan. This highly toxic little fellow is eaten raw and in soup and causes about three hundred poisoning deaths a year. Skillful chefs carry out a thirty-step process to remove the poison. But the best chefs let just enough poison remain to make the customer's lips tingle. Now that's real seafood dining satisfaction!

You can tune a guitar. You can tune a piano. Why not tuna steak?

More than three billion times a year, Americans reach for a can opener to enjoy their favorite fish. It's tuna, squeezed into a can the size of a hockey puck. Canned tuna has many advantages. You can stick it on a shelf and use it when you need it. Like most fish, it's nutrient-dense. It tastes good. And you can use the can as a hockey puck. Real tuna lovers, though, know there's life beyond the can. Fresh tuna, in a restaurant or fish market, makes a surprisingly good steak. It's cooked just like a beef steak—on a grill, under a broiler, or in a frying pan. Maybe with a little butter or steak sauce. Even real beef lovers ask for more. Some even think it's beef. And you don't need a can opener.

From the FOOD RULES! Dining Etiquette Handbook: Seafood should never be eaten with dirty hands. Eat dirty hands separately.

Bravery in the Face of Food

Adventure movies always seem to be about heroes achieving a goal while escaping vile villains and crazed animals. Real-life adventure is probably more about achieving a goal while eating weird food.

You may have heard about Ferdinand Magellan's crew being first to sail around the world. But did you know they ran out of food after only a few weeks and had to cook the ship's rats and eat wormy biscuits?

You've heard about Lewis and Clark exploring the American West. Wow. Nice rivers. What was *really* adventurous was when Lewis and Clark's crew got hungry and traded medicine for the native people's dogs. *And then they ate the dogs!* The natives thought these wacky explorers were completely disgusting!

When humans get lost and in trouble, they quickly stop being picky about food. The hypothalamus wants molecules, and anything goes. Ever look at an oyster? The outside looks like a rock. The inside looks like a lump of boogers. Do you suppose the first oysters were eaten during a cave family's elegant dinner party, or by some lost and starving soul who washed up on a beach? Today, of course, oysters are served at elegant dinner parties everywhere.

Every real survival guide includes a chapter or two about finding unusual foods in the wild. Who would think those pesky dandelion weeds could save a person's life? But the fact is that dandelion greens per gram have more calcium than milk, more potassium than bananas, and more vitamin A than just about any food in the world. Of course, the possibility of lawn chemicals makes it dangerous to eat just any dandelions. But when you're miles from civilization, a dandelion salad might just get you through another day of walking around in circles.

Snakes, lizards, frogs, and turtles can all be tasty treats when you're lost and hungry. In fact, many cultures consider them ordinary, everyday food. Remember to keep telling yourself, "It's all just molecules, it's all just molecules."

And next time you see one of those famous Warner Brothers cartoons, remember: *Both* the coyote and the roadrunner are edible when you need an emergency meal in the desert.

"Hey, Thanks for This Ugly, Wonderful Bird"

Ever take a good look at a real live turkey? It's weird. Lumpy red bags hanging down from its beak. Mottled-looking feathers. It walks like a dinosaur. When the hungry Pilgrims showed up in Massachusetts, they had never seen one before. But it didn't take long to fall in love with their tasty new friend. Within a year they were celebrating and giving thanks for turkeys, corn, and all kinds of brand-new (to them) foods that had helped them survive. It just goes to show—when at Plymouth Rock, do as the natives do.

Sweetbreads are neither sweet nor bread. They are the thymus glands of calves, pigs, or lambs, found near the throat. The French consider sweetbreads a gourmet food.

War Is Not Pretty

During the Siege of Paris in the 1870s, the French capital was cut off from food supplies for more than four months. As starvation set in, the citizens realized their zoo was like a big barnyard. Soon the Parisians were eating elephant, lion, giraffe, and zebra, and chasing down the local population of rats and cats. The French have long been known for their creativity with food. This time it may have saved their lives.

American Eats Bugs! Becomes Hero!

When a U.S. Air Force pilot was shot down in 1995, he managed to parachute into the farms and forests of Bosnia. For six days and nights he dodged enemy gunfire and slept covered in camouflage until he was picked up in a daring helicopter rescue. He had quite a story to tell the public, but everyone seemed interested in only one question: "Did you really eat *bugs?*" "Sure," he answered, "that's what the survival pamphlet said to do." And so Captain Scott O'Grady received a hero's welcome home and a spot on *The Tonight Show,* where he and Jay Leno showed the American public how to eat carpenter ants. (Warning: If the thought of eating bugs makes you antsy, you may want to skip the next chapter.)

From *FOOD RULES!* "Say-It-Out-Loud-Several-Times" Department

Why can't you starve in the desert?
Because of all the sand which is there.

Why was the baby cookie crying?
Because its mother had been a wafer so long.

Gopher Guts, Part 3
Great green globs of greasy, grimy gopher guts
Mutilated monkey meat
Nicely roasted, very sweet
All wrapped up in yummy purple porpoise pus
And I forgot my spoon!

Butterflies in Your Stomach

If aliens have encyclopedias, it's likely that humans are listed as insect eaters. That's because 80 percent of humans happily eat bugs as part of their everyday diets. The only places not yet comfortable with the idea of bug-based meals are the United States, Canada, Europe, and the polar regions. But that's likely to change. The nutrition in insects is just as good—and sometimes better—than the nutrition we get from grinding up huge animals. And far less messy, too.

In the world of science, people who eat bugs are called entomophagists (en-to-MA-fa-jists). Entomophagists are just about everywhere, scooping up pots full of termites in Africa, frying honeybees in Nepal, and crunching grasshoppers in Japan.

They're even in the schoolyard. You've probably heard nursery rhymes about hot cross buns and peas porridge cold. Well, if you were a Yansi child in central Zaire, Africa, your song might be a bit different:

Father, you must give me some millee caterpillars
Look at all the other kids with millee caterpillars
That their fathers gave them
I'm going to bother you until you give me some.

Across the South Atlantic, the Guayaki people of Paraguay don't wait for caterpillar season. Guayaki families knock down palm trees to make weevil farms. The trunks make perfect habitats for thriving herds of palm weevil grubs, some as large as mice. Next time you hear that breakfast griddle sizzling, think of this—roasted over hot coals, palm weevil grubs are said to taste very much like *bacon*!

In Mexico, some people get disappointed if ants *don't* show up at the picnic. There are restaurants in the city of Tlaxcoapan that charge 300 pesos for two tacos with 50 grams of ants fried with black butter. No need to worry about getting taco crumbs on the floor—extra ants are as welcome as you are!

China's answer to Burger King is Scorpion King. The big menu item at this fast-food chain is fried scorpions covered in ants. Hey, isn't a scorpion a lot like a lobster? Americans line up for the Friday-night King-O'-the-Sea All-You-Can-Eat Lobster Special, don't they? And did you ever take a good look at a live shrimp? It's a bug's cousin if ever there was one. It all depends on what you're used to. In most of the world, people are used to eating bugs.

Good and Good for You

A pound of termites, grasshoppers, caterpillars, or weevils has more high-quality protein than a pound of beef, chicken, pork, or lamb, says the Entomological Society of America. The fats found in insects are usually the "good" nonsaturated kind.

Relax, There's Plenty for Everyone

About 72 percent of all known living animals are classified as insects. The total weight of all insects on Earth has been estimated at twelve times the total weight of all humans. Termites and ants alone outweigh all mammals put together.

A sure way to see flying saucers is to trip a waiter.

A Delicious Meal(worm)

For its one hundredth anniversary, the New York Entomological Society held a buggy banquet. Tuxedo-clad waiters served more than a hundred guests a meal that included Peppery Delight Mealworm Dip, Roasted Australian Kurrajong Grubs, Sauteed Thai Water Bugs, and Chocolate Cricket Torte. The Associated Press reported that "diners found the crickets crunchy with a taste like mushrooms. The mealworms were chewy and tasted like fish. The ants tasted peachy and the waxworm fritters were nutty."

What Plague? It's Dinner

When insecticides failed to stop vegetable-hungry locusts in the Philippines, farmers finally got smart. The next time the critters appeared, the farmers began netting and selling them to city-dwellers as food. Soon bugs were selling like hotcakes, and locusts are now considered a gourmet's delight.

What does an aardvark like on its pizza? Ant-chovies.

The Granddaddy of American Bug-Eaters

When insect-eating catches on the United States (and it will), you can thank Dr. Gene R. Defoliart, professor emeritus of entomology at the University of Wisconsin. He spent decades studying and teaching about the benefits of insects as food. Since 1988, his *Food Insects Newsletter*, often quoted in the press, has been spreading the word about all that wiggly goodness out there.

Bugs Can Be Bad

No one should just go popping bugs into his or her mouth. Some insects make their own poisons, and others pick them up from the environment. Like a lot of foods (think uncooked hamburger and peanuts), bugs can also carry extremely unappetizing bacteria and parasites and can cause allergic reactions. In countries where insect-eating is common, people know just *what* bugs to eat, *how* to eat them, and *when* to eat them. If you're traveling to these countries and insects are on the menu, it's probably okay to try them. There are more and more American businesses dealing in food insects, including some that will send you boxes of buggy treats by mail-order. The point is, don't just pull a mess of grubs out of a stump in your backyard and start making sandwiches. . . .

Hey, Kids! Buy This!

It'll Make You Smarter, Cooler, Faster, Stronger, Better-Looking, and More Popular!

You're worth a lot of money. And not just those few bucks you have stuffed in your sock drawer. Every time you give your folks an idea about buying something—whether it's a bottle of soda or a loaf of bread—you're helping to control where the money goes.

Every year your ideas about what to eat and drink control how $80 *billion* get spent. And that's just American kids between the ages of four and twelve.

Because of all this money, food and drink companies love kids. Even more, they want you to love *them*. That's why they spend over $1 billion a year in advertising just to tell you how great, how cool, and how much fun their products are. By the time you're seventeen, you'll see at least 350,000 TV commercials!

Ever wonder what really goes on in college? Well, for one thing, they study the commercials on Saturday-morning kids' shows. Students found that more than half the commercials are trying to sell food products. *Way more* than half of *these* food commercials are trying to sell high-sugar cereal. Not once in fifty-two hours did any commercial try to sell vegetables or fruit.

Companies like to sell high-sugar cereal because it's easy to make, it lasts a long time on a store shelf, and most kids who taste the sugar say, "Ooh, that's good." It's your job to be sure the chyme you make from cereal is more than just sugar paste. Luckily, every box of cereal has a Nutrition-Facts label. That will tell you a lot more than a bunch of kids jumping around in a commercial.

When a commercial says something is *part* of a nutritious breakfast, they mean it. It's important to eat a wide variety of foods. If you just eat what the cool kids on TV eat, you'll make the food companies very happy. But you'll drive your hypothalamus insane!!!

The Dream We Eat for Breakfast
The first ready-to-eat flaked cereal (cornflakes) was invented by Dr. John Harvey Kellogg in 1894. He said the idea came to him in a dream.

Where Did All That Sugar Go?

Cereal makers used to attract kids by screaming SUGAR! SUGAR! SUGAR! on their boxes and in their commercials. The idea went sour in the 1970s when parents started *avoiding* foods with a lot of sugar. One by one all these cereals took "sugar" out of their names, changed their names completely, or went off the market. Today, many cereals still use the same amount of sugar (or more), but they don't name 'em like this anymore:

SUGAR SMACKS

SUGAR POPS

SUGAR-FROSTED FLAKES

SUGAR CRISP

SUGAR-SPRINKLED TWINKLES

SUGAR-FROSTED CORN BURSTS

SUGAR STARS

SUGAR-COATED CORNFLAKES

SUGAR-SPARKLED FLAKES

SUGAR-COATED RICE SPRINKLES

SUGAR CORN FETTI

SUGAR RICE KRINKLES

SUGAR PUFFS

SUGAR CHEX

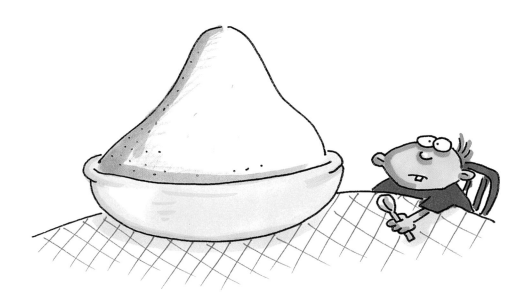

The Perfect Food

Wonder why your food never looks quite like the picture on the package? Well, maybe it's because you don't spend hours putting the food into the bowl. Food companies want perfect pictures on their packages. They hire people called food "stylists" who hand pick each and every cereal bit, pretzel, or potato chip that's in the picture. Sometimes they go through dozens of bags, looking for just the perfect shapes. Then, they spend hours, sometimes days, arranging the food. If it's cereal, they can't use milk because they'd have a soggy mess in minutes. Instead, they use tweezers to carefully place each cereal bit into a bowl of white vegetable shortening (like Crisco). Splashes? They're often just blobs of plastic. All the while, the photographer is adjusting lights and camera settings and arguing with the stylist. The fuss continues until the pictures are taken. And then the food is simply thrown away. It lives on, though, in pictures on boxes all across America, inspiring kids like you to make sad, soggy messes and wonder why.

What does a snowman love for breakfast?
Snowflakes.

We'll Eat It Tomorrow

Fruit that humans love but bugs hate. Growing your own vegetables year-round without soil. Taking your medicine by eating a banana. There are some changes coming in your eating habits—some are already here.

When agriculture began about 10,000 years ago, farmers quickly learned that planting seeds from the biggest, healthiest, best-tasting plants would make the next crop bigger, healthier, and better-tasting. And over the centuries they learned that pollen from one plant could change the seeds produced by another plant. But they didn't really know how it worked. For about ninety-nine centuries, producing better plants was strictly a matter of trial and error.

It wasn't until about 1900 that scientists really began to understand how genes—present in each cell of every living thing—pass traits such as size or ruggedness or flavor to the next generation of cells. In 1973, they learned how to add individual genes to cells. They can take a gene that helps make some melons big and a gene that helps make other melons sweet and add them to another melon that has a gene that helps make it distasteful to insects. By experimenting, the scientists could come up with a giant melon, sweet as candy, that bugs won't eat. Every melon farmer in the world would want some of this melon's seeds.

Moving individual genes from one living thing to another is called biotechnology (BY-oh-teck-naw-law-gee). It's also called genetic (jeh-NET-tick) engineering. By picking and choosing and moving genes around, scientists are beginning to develop food plants that resist bugs without pesticides, plants that thrive on less water and fertilizer, and plants that stay fresh longer after picking. They're making some vegetables bigger (giant corn!), some smaller (single-serving watermelon!), some more nutritious (super soybeans!), and some safer (allergy-free nuts!). And remember those ouchy vaccination shots? Kids may eventually get their vaccinations by eating biotechnology bananas!

Why did the cookie go to see the doctor?
He was feeling crummy!

We've Only Just Begun

It's said that biotechnology may become one of the biggest businesses of the twenty-first century. The U.S. Department of Agriculture has high hopes—greater amounts of crops with more nutritional value, grown in harsh climates using less water and pesticide, with less destruction of fragile lands and forests. Sounds great, and we've just started. The first biotechnology vegetable was sold in the United States in 1994. It was a tomato with genes engineered to help it keep its flavor longer.

Dirt? What Dirt?

Another technology that may change agriculture is hydroponics (hydro-PA-niks)—the science of growing plants without soil. Plants don't really need soil to grow. They need what's *in* the soil. It's quite possible to grow food plants in a mixture of water, nutrients, and minerals. By experimenting, scientists can adjust the mixture so it's exactly right for each individual crop. The result? Very little wasted water and fertilizer. And because hydroponic plants get everything they need, they tend to grow faster and bigger and need less space. What's more, hydroponic plants are easily grown indoors where light and temperature—and bugs—can be controlled. This makes it possible to grow food plants year-round, and without pesticides. Hydroponics has already been considered as a way to grow food during long space flights. In years to come, it may also become a common way for families to grow their own fresh vegetables year-round in basements or spare rooms.

"Hey, Sarah, run downstairs and pick me a big zucchini, will ya?"

The Food Rules! Festival of Fine Foods

Good Food Without Hot Stoves or Too Many Dirty Dishes

Pizza Sandwich

Mama mia, if real pizza were made like this, this would be just like real pizza! Toast two slices of whole-wheat bread in the toaster. (Okay, any bread will do, but whole wheat is better for you.) Put a slice of cheese and a slice of tomato in between the slices of bread. Put the sandwich on a microwave-safe plate and nuke it for about ten to twenty seconds (until the cheese is nicely melted). Before you eat it, make sure it's not hot enough to burn you.

Overnight Oatmeal

If you're going to want oatmeal for breakfast, just put about a half cup of ordinary, regular oatmeal in a bowl and add a half cup of milk. Mix it up and put it in the refrigerator before you go to bed. In the morning you'll have oatmeal. You can mix in flavorings if you like. You can eat it cold or put it in the microwave for a few seconds to warm it up.

Pink Cottage Cheese

Even people who don't think they like cottage cheese like *this* cottage cheese. Just spoon out how much you think you want into a bowl, add a few blobs of ketchup, and stir. Sounds weird, but it tastes great. Even weirder: This was one of President Gerald Ford's favorite foods.

Best Excuse for Midnight Snacking: Nocturnal Sleep-Related Eating Disorder (NS-RED) or eating while sleeping. NS-RED victims have been known to dunk hot dogs in peanut butter, eat raw bacon covered in mayonnaise, and slice soap and eat it like cheese.

All-Purpose Bean Dip

This is soooo simple. Just open a can of cooked beans. Pork 'n' beans
will work just fine. Dump out some, but not all, of the liquid. Dump the
beans and remaining liquid into a bowl and mash it all up with a fork
until it's smooth like a dip. Great for dipping crackers, carrots, celery,
and more. Makes an exquisite sandwich spread, too.

PB & B Sandwich

Don't eat this at the zoo. Both the monkeys and the elephants get very
jealous. Spread peanut butter on two slices of whole-wheat bread, or
whatever bread you have. Peel a ripe banana, slice it, and put the
banana slices between the pieces of bread. Magnificent.

No-Mystery Tuna Salad

Bet you never knew it was this easy. Open a can of tuna and drain out the liquid. Wash a piece of celery and slice it into little pieces. Put the drained tuna and the sliced celery into a bowl and plop in a few spoons of mayonnaise. Mix it around. You can eat this on bread, with crackers, or by itself.

No-Mystery Tuna Melt

Now we're getting advanced. Start by making the No-Mystery Tuna Salad, above. Then toast a slice of whole-wheat (or whatever) bread in the toaster. Spread the tuna salad on the bread and cover it with a piece of cheese. Put it on a microwave-safe plate and nuke it for ten to twenty seconds until the cheese is nicely melted. Before you eat it, make sure it's not hot enough to burn you.

Cockroaches Trapped in a Rain Gutter

Other books call these Ants on a Log. BO-ring. Las cucarachas are much more interesting. Just wash and dry celery stalks. Spread peanut butter into the celery groove. Stick raisins into the peanut butter. Enjoy, or just hide them under your dresser to attract real cockroaches and other household pests.

Why Go Hungry?

First-Class Passengers on the R.M.S. *Titanic*, April 14, 1912

A ten-course dinner including oysters, barley soup, salmon, cucumbers, filet mignon, chicken sauté, lamb with mint sauce, roast duckling, applesauce, beef sirloin, potatoes, peas, carrots, rice, roast pigeon, asparagus, goose liver, celery, pudding, peaches in chartreuse jelly, eclairs, and ice cream.

Richard Beavers, Death Row Prisoner, April 4, 1994

Six pieces of French toast, butter, syrup, jelly, six barbecued spare ribs, six strips of well-burned bacon, four scrambled eggs, five well-cooked sausage patties, French fries with ketchup, three slices of cheese, two pieces of yellow cake with chocolate-fudge icing, and four cartons of milk.

Elvis Presley, August 16, 1977

Four scoops of ice cream and six chocolate-chip cookies.

GLOSSARY

Allergy An unwanted reaction that certain substances, including food, can cause in some people.

Amino acids Chemical molecules that are the building blocks of protein. Digestion breaks down the protein you eat into amino acids.

Bile A greenish-yellowish liquid made by your liver, stored in your gall-bladder, and released into the beginning of your small intestine to help digest fats.

Biotechnology Also called *genetic engineering*. Moving, adding, or replacing genes to create changes in living things. Holds great promise in food production.

Blood vessels The body's nutrient superhighway. A 60,000-mile tangle of arteries, veins, and capillaries, it provides a way for nutrients to reach every cell of your body.

Bolus The lump of chewed-up food that goes down your throat and into your stomach.

Capsaicin The chemical in chili peppers that your brain mistakes for hot temperatures.

Carbohydrates The chemical substance in which plants store the energy from the sun. Your body gets all its energy from a simple carbohydrate called glucose.

Cholesterol A waxy substance made by the liver. It helps build and repair your body's cells, but too much can clog your arteries.

Chyme Food after your stomach liquefies it.

Diarrhea Watery feces that your body releases quickly when harmful bacteria are detected.

Digestion The process of breaking down food into molecules that the human body can use.

Entomologist A scientist who studies insects.

Entomophagist A human whose diet regularly includes insects. Eighty percent of the world's population are entomophagists.

Enzymes Proteins made in your body that help break down food substances and form the new molecules you need.

Fats Combinations of chemicals, called fatty acids, that have many functions in the body. Among other things, fats create body structures including the brain, help move messages around the brain, help the body use other nutrients, and store energy.

Feces What's left after the intestines have absorbed nutrients available in the chyme. Feces also contain the remains of bacteria, viruses, and old cells your body wants to eliminate.

Fiber Parts of plants your body can't turn into molecules. It moves all the way through the intestines, collecting debris and helping to make feces soft and easy to eliminate.

Flatulence The sound and smell of gas escaping from the final sphincter of the digestive system. The gas is produced by bacteria in your intestines helping you to digest your food. Sometimes known as "coughing in your pants" (describing the sound) and "cutting the cheese" (describing the smell).

Gallbladder Storage area for bile before it is released into the small intestine.

Gene Part of a code in each cell of a living thing that instructs the cell how to function. It can pass traits such as size or ruggedness or flavor to the next generation of cells.

Glucose This carbohydrate is the human body's only fuel. It can be broken down (digested) from other carbohydrates, stored in the liver or muscles, or converted from fats and protein. It is delivered to cells by the bloodstream.

Glycogen Glucose when it is stored in the liver and muscles.

Hunger The feeling of wanting to eat. Felt by different people in different ways.

Hydrochloric acid The strong acid in your stomach that helps dissolve food into chyme.

Hydroponics The science of growing plants in a mixture of water and nutrients instead of in soil.

Hypothalamus A small area in the middle of the brain that monitors many things about the blood, including the amount of nutrients it's carrying.

Liver A large organ with many functions. It makes bile and cholesterol; stores glucose as glycogen; helps the body use carbohydrates, proteins, fats, vitamins, and minerals; and makes, or tries to make, poisons harmless to the body.

Macronutrients Substances a body needs in relatively large amounts: carbohydrates, proteins, and fats.

Malnutrition Bad nourishment due to lack of food, eating the wrong balance of foods, or diseases that hurt the body's ability to use food.

Micronutrients Substances a body needs in relatively small amounts: vitamins and minerals.

Mineral A substance originally from the Earth's crust. Humans need about fifteen minerals in varying amounts for good health.

Molecule The smallest particle of a chemical substance that can still be identified as the substance—usually just a few atoms. Food must be broken down into molecules before your body can use it.

Mucus In the digestive system, a thick, gooey substance that helps protect the stomach walls from digestive juices.

Nutrient A substance in a food that a living thing can use, or break down and use.

Nutrition The process in which a living thing takes in, breaks down, and uses food for energy, growth, and repair.

Pancreas An important organ under the stomach that makes digestive juices for use in the small intestine. Outside of digestion, another part of the pancreas releases a substance called insulin into the blood to help control the amount of glucose flowing around.

Parasite A living thing that uses another living thing for nutrition but provides nothing good in return.

Proteins Various complex substances your body makes from amino acids. Thousands of different proteins are used throughout the body for building and repair. Enzymes are proteins that help break down and build other substances. Other proteins flow around in the blood, moving substances from spot to spot. If necessary, the body can convert protein into glucose for energy.

Saliva The first chemical of digestion. Lubricates food in your mouth and begins to break down carbohydrates.

Sphincter One of five muscular doorways in the digestive system.

Spoiled food Occurs when too many bacteria begin to eat and expel their wastes in food intended for humans or animals.

Sugar Carbohydrates that make things sweet and turn almost instantly into energy in your body.

Sulfur A smelly chemical that can be produced by bacteria feeding on the food you eat. Also present in onions and garlic.

Sweat Water released from your blood and through your skin to carry away extra body heat. Also called *perspiration*.

Taste A combination of messages the brain receives about the flavor of food. The messages come from our sense of smell and four types of taste buds on our tongues: sweet, salty, sour, and bitter. Some say there is a fifth taste called umami, a taste that's in mushrooms.

Thirst A feeling of dryness in the mouth that signals a need for water. The feeling is created completely in the brain.

Urine Not really a product of the digestive system. Urine is the body's liquid-waste product—mostly water and small amounts of substances like minerals and vitamins that your blood releases to keep chemical levels balanced in your body.

Vitamins Complex substances that help protein, carbohydrates, and protein do their jobs in the body. We need about thirteen different vitamins. Most are found in plants and animals, and we get most of them by eating food.

Water Often overlooked as a nutrient, water is the most common substance in the body. Without water, nothing else works.

SELECT BIBLIOGRAPHY

Berkow, Robert, ed. *The Merck Manual of Diagnosis and Therapy, 15th Edition.* Rahway, N.J.: Merck & Co., 1987.

Branzei, Sylvia. *Grossology, The Science of Really Gross Things!* Reading, Mass.: Planet Dexter, 1995.

Burnie, David. *The Concise Encyclopedia of the Human Body.* New York: DK Publishing, 1995.

Chalmers, Irena. *The Great Food Almanac: A Feast of Facts from A to Z.* San Francisco: Collins Publishers, 1994.

Cobb, Vicki. *Science Experiments You Can Eat.* Philadelphia and New York: J.B. Lippincott Company, 1972.

Duyff, Roberta Larson. *The American Dietetic Association's Complete Food & Nutrition Guide.* Minneapolis: Chronimed Publishing, 1996.

Elfman, Eric. *Almanac of the Gross, Disgusting & Totally Repulsive.* New York: Random House, 1994.

Geisel, Theodore S. and Geisel, Audrey S. *Green Eggs and Ham.* New York: Random House, 1960.

Gilbert, Sara D. *You Are What You Eat.* New York: Macmillan Publishing, 1977.

Jaeger, Ellsworth. *Wildwood Wisdom.* New York: Macmillan Company, 1945.

Ontario Science Center. *Foodworks: Over 100 Science Activities and Fascinating Facts That Explore the Magic of Food.* Reading, Mass.: Addison-Wesley Publishing, 1987.

Parker, Steve. *Shocking Science: 5000 Years of Mishaps and Misunderstandings.* London: Hamlyn Children's Books, 1996.

Patent, Dorothy Hinshaw. *Nutrition: What's in the Food We Eat.* New York: Holiday House, 1992.

Schwabe, Calvin W. *Unmentionable Cuisine.* Charlottesville, Va.: University Press of Virginia, 1979.

Shils, M.E., J.A. Olson, M. Shike, A.C. Ross, eds. *Modern Nutrition in Health and Disease, 9th Edition.* Baltimore: Williams & Wilkins, 1999.

Solheim, James. *It's Disgusting and We Ate It! True Food Facts from Around the World and Throughout History!* New York: Simon & Schuster, 1998.

INDEX